HIDE ME

(A Katie Winter FBI Suspense Thriller—Book 3)

Molly Black

Molly Black

Bestselling author Molly Black is author of the MAYA GRAY FBI suspense thriller series, comprising nine books (and counting); the RYLIE WOLF FBI suspense thriller series, comprising six books (and counting); of the TAYLOR SAGE FBI suspense thriller series, comprising three books (and counting); and of the KATIE WINTER FBI suspense thriller series, comprising six books (and counting).

An avid reader and lifelong fan of the mystery and thriller genres, Molly loves to hear from you, so please feel free to visit www.mollyblackauthor.com to learn more and stay in touch.

ISBN: 978-1-0943-9462-6

BOOKS BY MOLLY BLACK

MAYA GRAY MYSTERY SERIES
GIRL ONE: MURDER (Book #1)
GIRL TWO: TAKEN (Book #2)
GIRL THREE: TRAPPED (Book #3)
GIRL FOUR: LURED (Book #4)
GIRL FIVE: BOUND (Book #5)
GIRL SIX: FORSAKEN (Book #6)
GIRL SEVEN: CRAVED (Book #7)
GIRL EIGHT: HUNTED (Book #8)
GIRL NINE: GONE (Book #9)

RYLIE WOLF FBI SUSPENSE THRILLER
FOUND YOU (Book #1)
CAUGHT YOU (Book #2)
SEE YOU (Book #3)
WANT YOU (Book #4)
TAKE YOU (Book #5)
DARE YOU (Book #6)

TAYLOR SAGE FBI SUSPENSE THRILLER
DON'T LOOK (Book #1)
DON'T BREATHE (Book #2)
DON'T RUN (Book #3)

KATIE WINTER FBI SUSPENSE THRILLER
SAVE ME (Book #1)
REACH ME (Book #2)
HIDE ME (Book #3)
BELIEVE ME (Book #4)
HELP ME (Book #5)
FORGET ME (Book #6)

PROLOGUE

Jon Farrow stopped at the branch in the path and turned to his wife. He was breathing fast, his legs aching. Despite the freezing temperatures, sweat was trickling down his back.

The great outdoors? You could keep it, he thought.

This snowshoeing was a lot more effort than he'd expected. The brochure and video had made it look fun and easy. But, surrounded by snow-packed trees, the trail was narrow, and he had to concentrate to avoid the deep ruts. The snowshoes kept him from sinking, but his thighs burned as he plodded forward.

"That way leads us back to the chalets," he pointed meaningfully down the hill.

"And that way leads us over the ridge," his wife argued, raising a gloved hand and pointing in the opposite direction. Lydia's blond hair, as icy pale as the snow, framed her face under the knit cap, and the weak sunshine sparkled off the diamonds in her earrings.

"We've only been going for half an hour," she argued, removing her glove, consulting her Fitbit. "I've only burned two hundred and thirty-three calories so far. Let's get it up to a round four hundred at least."

He sighed, annoyed.

"I'm tired," he said. "And I have a call with a supplier at eleven a.m."

Business was business, regardless of being on vacation or not. Money had to be made.

As if she hadn't heard him, she continued, "That lobster and Wagyu dinner last night was a heavy meal. And we flattened nearly a bottle of Moet each. We need to work it off."

Playfully, she poked him in the gut before replacing her glove.

With a frustrated sigh, Jon turned to follow her. He could be on vacation in Cancun now, watching the sea from beside the pool and drinking iced margaritas. Would have been, if their neighbors hadn't vacationed on a luxury ranch, and given her this wild idea about a winter getaway.

He turned to follow, his legs aching as he stumbled through the snow.

The path they'd been following was a lot narrower now. It had been forged across the hilltop; at the ridge line it was little more than a foot wide. He slid a little as he tried to step off the path, dipping his foot into the snow.

He swore.

The path, and the ridge, led to that sharp slope he'd been skirting. They'd been doing a lot of that; avoiding steep drops, trying not to look into the valleys below.

"Maybe we should turn around now."

"It's fine!" she called back to him.

"It isn't!"

But she was already out of reach, her footsteps crunching and slipping away from him.

The path narrowed further as it neared the edge of the ridge.

"Hey! Hang on!" This wasn't just torturous. It was dangerous, too. The slope to the left looked sharp and rugged.

"We just need to keep going a little bit further," she called.

"This is stupid! We're not snowshoeing. We're mountain climbing!"

She didn't answer.

Jon fumed, watching her large, flat footprints move steadily away from him.

Glancing one last time down at the slope, he noted it was a long way down. And he didn't even know how to get back to the chalets.

He swore under his breath. It was too late.

He took a tentative step forwards, onto the ridge. And then, the worst happened. The snow crumbled away from under him as he fell.

Yelping in fright, he scrambled for something to grab onto, but there was nothing. He landed on the snowy incline, and began to slide.

He tried to reach for a sapling, jutting out of the snow, but its stem whipped out of his grasp.

Gasping, Jon slid to a stop at the bottom of the ridge. The snow settled over him, showering him. He blinked, but he couldn't see anything beyond the powdery white.

"Lydia!" he shouted, but all he could hear was the wailing wind.

A moment later, his wife's face appeared at the top of the ridge, framed by her white earmuffs.

"Jon! Are you okay?"

She didn't sound anxious. More amused.

He could have broken something. Probably had. That would teach her, if he'd suffered a real injury thanks to her stupid ideas. Jon moved his arms and legs.

To his disappointment, all were in working order.

His gloved hand knocked against something.

A snowshoe. His shoe must have come off in the fall.

But to Jon's confusion, he saw both his shoes were still attached.

He tried to pull the spare shoe clear, vaguely wondering why it felt so heavy.

And then, Jon cried out as he saw the snowshoe was attached to a foot.

His heart dropped.

Someone else must have fallen down this slope. And not been as lucky as him.

Suddenly, this remote outdoors didn't just feel cold and inhospitable. It felt actively dangerous.

Jon was shaking all over now, from the stress of the fall and from this horrific discovery. The body felt icy cold. Whatever had happened, he feared this man was beyond help.

He reached out, and with trembling fingers, brushed snow from the face of the corpse.

The face was covered in cuts and slices and the head was at an unnatural angle, but it was the victim's neck that caught Jon's horrified attention.

The man's throat had been torn open. Blood was frozen across the ruptured skin.

Jon didn't think it could get any worse. But as he stared at the man's pale, ruined face, it did.

This was one of their fellow vacationers. Just a few hours ago, they'd greeted each other over the breakfast buffet. He'd shared a glance of commiseration with the guy, sensing that both of them were at this overpriced resort because of their wives.

"Lydia!" he shouted, again and again, his shouts drowned out by the wind.

Jon began scrambling up the slope, shaking violently, and chilled with a fear that pierced even deeper than the snowy cold.

“Lydia!”

CHAPTER ONE

Katie Winter stood outside the small house that had been her childhood home, feeling memories engulf her as she knocked at the front door.

At the age of thirty-two, she'd been an FBI agent for over six years, handling some of the toughest and most dangerous serial killer cases. She'd been in close-quarter gunfights and escaped abduction by psychotic murderers.

But at this moment, she didn't feel brave. She felt alone and scared. She was afraid to go inside that house again, and try to break the silence between herself and her parents after so many long years of estrangement.

Memories flared, as she vividly recalled standing at this same door at the age of sixteen, after the tragedy with her twin sister. Feeling exhausted, chilled and devastated, her brown hair had been dripping from the river water and her face had been wet with tears. When the door had opened, she'd broken the news to her parents that Josie, was gone. Disappeared after a kayaking accident that had been Katie's fault. She should never have gone out on the river, in such wild conditions.

Since then, her parents had been estranged from her. They blamed her, Katie knew. That was understandable. She blamed herself, too.

Nerves twisted her stomach at the thought of what might play out between herself and her parents. She wasn't a fearful person normally. She was known for her icy cool under pressure at work, and could face down any danger with a calm mind and steady hands.

But the trauma of her family past reduced her to a shaking wreck.

What was happening now? There was no answer to her knock. Were her parents even inside? She thought they were. She could hear the TV. So what was going on?

Tiptoeing around to the side of the wooden home, Katie peeked through the window.

Her dad was there. She could see his silhouette against the flickering orange light of the television, as he sat in his favorite armchair, feet up on the battered old coffee table, a hot drink in one hand. Beside him, her mother sat in the chair to his left.

She was shocked by how they looked.

Her father had always been a big, strong man, a rugged outdoorsman with a bushy mustache and a face that showed evidence of the harsh conditions he'd endured, out on the lake in all weathers with his boat hire company.

Now, his face looked drawn, and his hair was very gray. He seemed more shrunken than she remembered.

Her mother was a naturally slender woman, but she seemed to have lost a lot of weight. Her face, once pretty, was now lined, and her eyes had dark circles under them.

Katie's heart ached. She remembered how her mother had always been a strong, determined woman, despite the tough life she'd had to endure, scraping out a living through tourism and boat hire in this small town. She'd always been such a warm person, with a big smile on her face, making the most of what she had.

And now, that was gone. Her mother looked like an empty shell.

"No! You can't do this! I won't allow this! You need to let me back in," the woman on the TV screamed, her voice shrill. The words resonated with Katie and she shivered.

That was the only sound in the room. Her parents seemed trapped in a silence that neither could escape from. They were not even speaking to each other.

Katie glanced at the empty seat to her mother's right. Now unoccupied for sixteen years, that small chair still held her twin's ghostly shadow.

They must have heard the knock on the door. But Katie's father just sat there, his eyes on the TV screen. He didn't seem to have noticed his daughter outside.

Swallowing, she took a deep breath, and tried to keep her face impassive. She didn't want to look as though she was about to break down, although she could feel emotions bubbling up beneath the surface.

She had so much to say to them, but now she wondered if they had anything to say to her at all.

Katie turned and glanced at the small, scrubby garden at the side of the house, noticing that the old swing had been removed. She remembered how it had creaked in the wind at night. She'd always found the sound comforting.

Now, nothing about this environment seemed to offer any comfort or hope.

Turning back, she tapped softly on the window, not wanting to startle them, but needing them to know she was here.

She'd had plenty of time in the years since she'd left home, to think of scenarios that might play out if she came back one day to confront her estranged parents. And she'd used the time to think about what she was going to say, to herself as much as to her family.

But this wasn't going the way she'd expected. It was as if they couldn't hear her.

Briefly, Katie wondered if this was what it felt like to be a ghost. The sensation was creepy. She wondered if they could see her at all. Surely they had heard the noise, and noticed the movement from outside, darkening the brightness of snow on sun that streamed through the glass into the gloomy house?

But her father just stared at the window, blankly. Surely he must see her.

And yet he didn't appear to recognize his daughter. It was as though she was a stranger.

He turned and stared back at the flickering TV screen blankly, like a zombie.

Her mother glanced over, and looked straight past her - as if she hadn't noticed Katie there. As if she didn't see the woman who'd spent the past sixteen years of her life hoping desperately to be accepted and forgiven - by them, if not herself.

Katie's heart pounded hard. Sixteen years ago, it had been the same as today. They had ignored her, too. This was why she had left. After their initial furious anger, their grief over Josie had been so great that they had simply stopped interacting with her. And now, they were doing it again.

She didn't even know if it was a deliberate attempt to hurt her, or whether they were just trying to shield themselves from the confrontation they never wanted to have.

Katie had come here, hoping to be able to talk to them. To explain. To try and find a way back. But she should have known better.

She was nothing to them now.

Pain clenched at her. She wanted to yell that it hadn't been her fault, that it had been a moment of youthful recklessness.

If the known serial killer Charles Everton hadn't been in that area when Josie's kayak capsized, she would have found her way home again and everything would have been alright again.

Or so Katie suspected.

She'd always believed Everton had murdered Josie, even though the killer had denied it when police had arrested him during the search.

But a couple of weeks ago, when she'd come face to face with him in the maximum-security prison where he was serving his time, Everton had taunted her, saying that Josie was the one who begged him to save her. She was the one he never killed.

Katie had no idea what he'd meant by that. It had been one of the things she'd wanted to talk to her parents about, and to ask if they knew. If there was anything in this painful tragedy that they had known but hadn't told.

Her stomach roiled with the same sense of entrapment and helplessness that she'd felt sixteen years ago.

Her mother looked back at the flickering TV screen. Her dad didn't even seem to have noticed her, still staring at the picture, and holding that mug.

She'd always feared this outcome, deep down.

Nothing had changed in the time since she'd left, except her.

She'd wanted to come back here and sort it all out. To try and get back the sense of peace that had been shattered so long ago.

She'd wanted to be forgiven. Needed to be forgiven. She'd wanted to be able to move on with her life, and to reconcile with her parents.

But, as she'd always feared, they didn't want to see her. It was as if, in that tragedy, both their daughters had died.

Katie turned away, wiping away a tear.

She was nothing to them now.

CHAPTER TWO

It was a chilly Sunday, Detective Leblanc's first day off in a long time, but instead of relaxing, he was using the time to revisit a part of his past he would rather have forgotten.

He was seated at the desk in his small apartment in Sault Ste Marie, the city on the St Mary's river that straddled Canada and the US and had therefore been chosen as the base for the cross-border task force that he was part of.

This city, originally a fur trading post and later the base for the steel and logging industries, had shrunk in size when the industries had downscaled. However, thanks to its magnificent location and plentiful snow, it had reinvented itself as a tourist destination, appealing to lovers of the outdoors.

Leblanc had promised himself to take a walk down the main street later, seeing the snow had stopped and weak sunshine was spilling through the window.

But for now, he was obsessing again about the case that had derailed his life a few years ago, when he'd been working in Paris.

He remembered how, when he'd first joined the police force, he'd been so idealistic. He remembered how he'd wanted to make a difference, to put wrongs to rights, to be the good guy fighting the bad. And he'd been paired up with someone who was just as passionate about justice as he was.

His investigation partner, Cecile Roux, had also become his lover. The two of them had been so close. Leblanc remembered her vividly.

Cecile's eyes had danced with laughter when she'd been in a good mood, sparkling when she was tender, and darkening when she was angry. Her black hair tumbled past her shoulders, caressing her cheeks, and her mouth was as full as an angel's.

He remembered the way she used to walk into a room, brisk and authoritative but with an air of compassion behind her sternness. He recalled how her voice had sounded as she told him how much she loved him. She used to take his hand and squeeze it, a gesture that had sent shivers up his spine.

The pain of her loss still haunted him. She'd gone into a prison to interview a suspect on her own. A riot had broken out and she'd been stabbed. He hadn't been there to help her. Leblanc knew he could have tried to save her, but he'd been delayed, and because of that, he'd lost the most important person in his life.

He'd broken the rule that they always went into a potentially risky situation together. With recent riots having erupted there, that prison had been a risky environment.

Leblanc glanced at the window, seeing his own reflection against the glass. His crisply cut dark hair, his pale olive skin, the expression of pain in his dark eyes.

A shadow passed across the window, blotting out the image of his reflection.

Leblanc looked up, and saw the silhouette of a large bird sailing past. An eagle, or maybe a hawk. It landed on the limb of a tree outside his first-floor apartment.

For a moment, he felt as though it was looking back at him, silently challenging him to atone for the tragedy of Cecile's death, even though he knew it was impossible.

He felt a pang of guilt, swiftly followed by anger at his inability to move on. This isn't just about me, he thought.

Now, he had a new investigation partner. He was working in a different place. This was his chance to restart his life and go forward afresh, but already, Leblanc worried that he was blurring the boundaries, and setting himself up for pain and heartbreak.

He'd suggested to Katie Winter that they reopen the case file that had gone cold after her twin's disappearance.

Although he wanted to help her, to earn her trust and vice-versa, he was afraid of getting to know her.

He was scared they would get too close.

Relooking at such an old case would be difficult and he knew that it might reawaken demons that were better left undisturbed.

But there was something about Katie Winter that made him want to help her in any way he could.

Her toughness. Her courage and resolve. Her icy professionalism that seldom wavered. She was strong, despite her slender build. Her green eyes could blaze with anger when she was in a temper.

He told himself, stubbornly, that he was not doing this because he was still in love with the memory of his lost partner, but because he believed in justice. And because, if anything was going to help Katie move on, it was the chance to find out what happened to her sister.

He wanted to help her find out the full truth.

Deep in thought, Leblanc jumped when his phone shrilled from the bedroom.

He hurried through to the small, neat room, which he'd decorated with prints of Paris. Surprisingly, being able to look at the landmarks he remembered so well - the Eiffel Tower, the Champs Elysees, Notre Dame - brought him comfort rather than sadness.

Grabbing the phone, he saw to his surprise that it was the task force leader, Detective Scott, on the line.

This could only mean one thing, Leblanc thought, excitement surging inside him as he took the call.

"Good morning, Scott," he said.

"Leblanc. We have just been notified that a body has been found on a ranch in northern Montana," Scott said, his voice crisp and unemotional as he presented the concise facts.

Surprised by how far west this case was, Leblanc glanced at the map on his desk where the task team's jurisdiction was highlighted. Sure enough, it covered the entire length of the border, with an overlap of a hundred miles or so in each direction. So this was something they could take on.

"Suspicious circumstances?" Leblanc asked, thinking they surely must be for Scott to have made this call.

"Yes. The body was found on the Diamond Ice Ranch, a luxury ranch in Montana that caters for a high-end clientele. The victim is Chris Banks, who with his wife, was a guest at the ranch. He was accounted for at breakfast time, and went out afterward. His body was found mid-morning."

"How was his body found?"

"Another guest stumbled upon it, literally. He slipped off the pathway while snowshoeing and fell onto it. Chris Banks was dead, with marks on his face and his throat slashed."

Immediately, Leblanc's detective brain went into overdrive.

"Are you sure it's a murder?" he asked, thinking that Banks could have fallen, and then potentially have been mauled by a wild animal before, or shortly after, his death.

"It's early days yet, but the coroner who attended the scene called us as he suspected otherwise," Scott said. "Plus, there's an additional complication. This isn't the first case of this type. There was a similar one, a week or so ago, at a ranch near Maple Creek in Canada. As soon as I got this notification, Detective Clark and I looked back and found the previous case. Having these two so similar is too much of a coincidence."

"Wait a minute. I remember seeing that report come up last week on the feed in our offices," Leblanc said. "It was a woman, wasn't it? And her body was found a couple of days after she disappeared, at the bottom of a ravine."

"Correct. Because that body was partially decomposed, they eventually put it down to a combination of a fall causing the death, and predators mauling the body. But there was also a neck wound, and other similarities align. She was also a wealthy tourist, vacationing at a ranch. I've been in touch with the Maple Creek authorities, to compare notes in more detail, and they're sending me the information shortly."

"Any more details about this second case?" Leblanc asked.

"No. But I don't want to waste a moment. I'm putting you and Katie Winter in charge of this, because Clark and Anderson have just been assigned to a cash-in-transit heist near the Niagara Falls border."

Leblanc felt eager to be working with Katie. They made a damned good team.

"I can be ready to go immediately," Leblanc said, glancing at his laptop bag. He always kept a change of clothes and a spare toothbrush in there, to be prepared for exactly this eventuality.

He'd been to Montana before and he loved the state's wilderness. He'd never heard of the Diamond Ice ranch, but knew that there were many successful ranch businesses operating on both sides of the US Canada border.

A suspected serial killing would devastate these businesses, which relied on the thrill of the wild open spaces to tempt their high-profile guests. He was sure these killings would result in immediate political pressure to solve the crime.

"There's a charter plane leaving for Havre, Montana, in an hour, so get to the airport as soon as you can. As I'm sure you can imagine, we're under the gun with this one. The ranch owners in both countries are already in contact with their various authorities, demanding that this is solved."

"You can count on us," Leblanc said.

"I'm sending you and Katie a dossier with all the details about the case. Call me if you need anything else," Scott said. "This is one you'll need to be on top of. I'm heading into a meeting now. I've just messaged both of you the flight details, and Katie has acknowledged, but if you could call her and give her the brief background I've given you, that would be great."

"I will do. And we'll do our best," Leblanc said.

"Do more than that. The pressure will be on from the minute you get there," Scott said. "Good luck."

Hurriedly, Leblanc called a cab, while packing a few more items into a travel bag, and threw on some warm clothing. As he left the building, he pictured Katie, her quick response, her sharp insight.

Leblanc couldn't wait to get to the Diamond Ice Ranch and get started on the case right away. Especially seeing, with a serial killer, every hour that passed brought the risk that he might strike again.

While waiting for the cab, he dialed Katie's number, ready to brief her on their newest challenge.

CHAPTER THREE

Katie climbed into her seat in the small charter plane, feeling a sense of anticipation about the investigation ahead. She knew it was thanks to her past that this type of case unleashed an iron-hard determination within her to catch the monster committing these serial crimes. She pushed back a stray lock of her brown hair, fastening it in the bun she liked to wear for work.

To her, the killer presented a grave threat to the security of every single person visiting those top-end ranches. It took just one person's predatory and twisted mind to set off a sequence of events that could result in the deaths of so many.

The flight wasn't a long one. They would fly direct to Havre, Montana. From there, the local police would meet them and drive them out to the ranch itself. She felt glad to be busy with a case, after the debacle of visiting her parents the day before. Before Leblanc had called, she'd been agonizing over what to do next. She wasn't going to give up, that she knew, but she felt temporarily daunted after the gut-wrenching hurt of being ignored by them.

At that moment, she saw her investigation partner climb into the plane. Leblanc's solemn expression brightened when he saw her.

"Going to be an interesting case," he said, without any preliminaries.

Katie liked his directness, although she was the first to admit that it sometimes strayed into the territory of arrogance. They'd struck sparks off each other the first time they'd worked together. Then, on their next case, she'd nearly compromised their relationship by not being open about her past, and what had happened to Josie.

But since then, with their issues all on the table and a better understanding of each other, Katie realized they complemented each other. They had a balanced dynamic. She was analytical and cool, he was quick and decisive.

And, more than that, as a person he was smart, tenacious, and committed.

"It will be a challenge. I'm pleased we're on it so early. I hope we can get a quick lead on what's happening."

Leblanc nodded. "I'm glad to be working with you on it."

"Likewise," Katie said, meaning it.

A few moments later, the engines started up, and they began to taxi along the runway. It took off, and the two of them spent a few moments in companionable silence.

Glancing out of the window, Katie took a look at the view below. The trip was taking them due west, and from the window, she could see the dark, icy waters of Lake Superior below, with thick forests and swathes of wilderness beyond.

She had a love-hate relationship with the harsh terrain in this northerly region, close to where she'd grown up. The land was beautiful and green in summer, with the majestic lake shores and the great pine forests.

But when it came to winter, this terrain could be like a bleak, frozen hell. A wasteland ravaged by blizzards and cut off from civilization.

Even in the spring, when the winter snow melted and the ground thawed, the region could be hit by unseasonably heavy rains that flooded farmlands.

Again, the image of the river loomed in her mind. The ride through the boiling rapids where her twin had gone missing would forever be imprinted in her memories and nightmares.

Turning away from the window, angry with herself for her loss of focus, Katie opened the dossiers on the Diamond Ice Ranch case and the earlier one, the Maple Ranch case, that Scott had sent them. Inside, she found her first impression confirmed. This was going to be a challenging investigation.

On the one hand, there were a lot of similarities between the two victims. Both were wealthy tourists visiting cold weather locations. Both were married. They were both visiting ranch businesses, which catered to a high-end clientele and promised every luxury.

On the other hand, however, there were some small differences. The Canadian victim, Elaine Malanchuk, had been found by a search party a couple of days after she'd failed to return from a hike in the grounds. Given the harsher terrain in which her body had been discovered, they'd put the death down to a fall into the ravine and the large wound down to a scavenger. Now it seemed otherwise. There were too many similarities and too few differences for this to be coincidence.

Katie turned to Leblanc, and said, "I think we've got a serial killer on our hands."

"I agree," Leblanc said.

"It will mean a lot of pressure to solve this one quickly," Katie said.

"In this case, the location might actually work in our favor. We should have the full cooperation of the Canadian authorities. We'll also have full cooperation from the local ranch owners, who will be desperate to get this resolved before it affects business," Leblanc said.

"I'm sure it already has," Katie said grimly.

"True."

"A serial killer is big news. Especially if wealthy guests are being targeted. This is going to get a lot of attention, and the problem is that the media coverage might affect his killing patterns. Or hers, of course, it could be a woman doing this. He or she might end up killing faster due to the increasing pressure," Katie said.

"Do you think that will happen?" Leblanc asked.

"It's possible, yes. A public investigation and a media furor will make people more aware, but it also makes the situation more dangerous," Katie said regretfully.

"Do we have any idea what the weapon could be?" Leblanc asked. "I glanced at the photographs, and those wounds are weird. They did look like an animal attack. I can't blame them for deciding that was how the first victim died."

"No. I hope we can get more information on the weapon when we arrive," Katie said.

A few moments later, the airplane started its descent. Katie took a look at the time. It was two-thirty p.m. They'd made pretty good time, and were well ahead of schedule.

As the plane touched down, her heart beat a little faster. She knew that this would be a challenging case, but one that had the potential to go either way. For the investigators, and for the lives of anyone else who might be the killer's next target.

This local airport in the far north of Montana was nothing more than a strip of blacktop and a few outbuildings and warehouses. A police vehicle was waiting on the blacktop.

Leblanc and Katie filed out of the plane, descended the stairs, and headed straight for the police car.

In the driver's seat, Katie saw a middle aged man with neatly trimmed blond hair, wearing a police uniform.

"Hello, I'm Deputy Chief Darrell Waters," the man said. "I'm the assistant to the local police chief. You're Agent Winter and Detective Leblanc from the task force?"

Katie nodded, pleased by his efficiency.

"That's right," Leblanc said.

"Glad to have you here. I know you're going to be a big help with this case," Waters said. "This has shaken everyone. Our office has been inundated with calls. We're used to accidental deaths out here, but murders - well, they hardly ever occur. Most often, when they do, it's a domestic violence incident, or alcohol-related fights," he said somberly. "There are a few folk who still believe it's an animal attack and that it can be explained away. But other than that, there's a lot of panic among the community."

"I think we should start by going straight to the crime scene," Katie said.

She wanted to get a feel for the place, and take a look at the terrain and surroundings where the killer had struck. It would be the first step to learning about his thought processes and logic. She knew that if they were going to solve this case successfully, they would need to get all the way inside the mind of the person who had committed these brutal murders.

CHAPTER FOUR

As the police car slowed outside the main gates of Diamond Ice Ranch, Leblanc stared at the facade with reluctant admiration.

The ranch was a sprawling luxury resort, with a main building in the center and chalets spread out among knots of trees, with paths leading to them. From the paved driveway outside the main gates, a neatly kept roadway ran in a wide circle to the various other outbuildings.

Wooden fences, painted white, ran in straight lines through the grounds, like the spokes of a wheel, with one main entrance.

A small hangar was set behind the entrance gates, and a helipad and parking lot were located to the right of the main mansion. Several SUVs and luxury cars were parked there.

The lawn in front of the mansion was wide. Lightly dusted with snow, it had well-kept flower beds on either side of the steps leading to the porch. In the center of the lawn, a large stone statue of a rearing horse provided a focal point.

The building was a big, white, colonial style palace, with two stories, and a wide flight of stairs leading up to a front porch. The doors and windows were a deep, dark green.

This is the main building," Waters said. "It's the center of the resort. It has the reception, the restaurant, the bar, the spa and the indoor pool. The other buildings are the other guest chalets."

Leblanc stared at the scene before him, impressed with the beauty of the place.

As they climbed out of the car, they saw a young woman in a uniform approaching them.

"Good afternoon, I'm Jessica, one of the receptionists here," the young woman said. "How can I help you?"

"Hello, Jessica. I'm Agent Winter, and this is Detective Leblanc," Katie said, introducing them both.

Jessica nodded solemnly.

"We're so glad to have you here. This is such a terrible thing. I mean, we're all devastated about the guest being killed, but it's like everyone is blaming our ranch, as if we should have somehow stopped it happening. Blaming us. It's awful. And they're leaving, threatening never to come back. We've already had three groups of guests check out early, and another group has already canceled. Every day that passes is going to be more disastrous for us."

"I hope we can help you quickly," Leblanc agreed.

Katie nodded sympathetically at Jessica, realizing she was probably shouldering a lot of unpleasantness as guests took out their fear and anger on her.

Waters cleared his throat. "Can you organize for all of us to head out to the scene where it happened? These specialist investigators would like to view it."

"Of course. I'll get a porter to take your bags inside meanwhile, and one of our ranch hands will drive you to the - the place where it happened. Are you sure we can't offer you tea, coffee, a glass of sherry first?"

"Thanks, but we'd better get straight to work," Leblanc said.

She pulled out her phone and made a quick call. In only a minute, a large SUV pulled around the side of the building. It was painted dark green, with a white and gold logo emblazoned on the side.

It was driven by a young, clean-cut man wearing a green parka and a straw-colored cowboy hat. He looked solemn and stressed, but in spite of that, had a professional air.

"Good afternoon," he said, jumping out and opening the other doors.

Leaving Katie to get in the front, Leblanc climbed in the back with Waters.

The driver pulled off, heading along the paved road, through a large loop and into a straight road that led to the back of the property.

The magnificent landscape of the ranch greeted them. The long, white fences, the snowy fields, and the sweeping mountains in the distance.

The ranch hand headed out on the paved road. After driving for about half a mile, he turned right and the heavy vehicle bumped over a snowy track.

They were heading into a forested area. The track wove through trees, and branches heavy with snow brushed the roof.

Katie spotted a deer near the road, frozen in fear. It looked at them with big, wide eyes, and then bounded off when they were close.

The SUV moved deeper into the forest, between the trees and past bushes that were covered in white frost. Then the ranch hand stopped the car.

"We can't drive further as the track is too narrow, but it's been well trampled down. You okay to walk a hundred yards or so?"

The forest had thinned, and ahead was a high ridge, with a steep but short slope on the side of the track.

"Sure," Leblanc said, after glancing at Katie.

They climbed out of the car, with Waters bringing up the rear.

Walking along the slope, they followed the trail of crushed foliage and broken snow.

"It's here," Waters said, pointing to the edge of the slope. "The body was removed earlier. We do have photos of the scene, which I can show you now."

Leblanc looked around, and then down.

Although the slope was moderate, it wasn't far to the bottom and he didn't see that anyone could have fallen to their death down it. Not unless they had been very frail.

"How old was the victim?" he asked, wanting to rule that out.

"Chris Banks was forty-five. He and his wife were on day five of a week's stay and they had been out every day. He wasn't in great shape, but even so, he was enjoying the outdoors."

"Why didn't she go with him today?" Leblanc asked.

"I'm not sure," Waters said.

Leblanc filed that away as being potentially suspicious.

They still couldn't rule out that one of the two victims might have died in another way, he thought. All possible scenarios needed to be considered. Leblanc was not convinced that this was a serial murder. Not yet. Even though he knew Katie was sure, Leblanc himself needed more hard evidence to persuade him before he reached that conclusion.

"Can I see the photos?" he asked.

"Sure."

Waters opened his backpack and took out a laptop. He opened it up and they crowded around the screen, their breath misting in the cold air.

He opened up the file of photos of the crime scene. Leblanc looked over them.

Lying at the bottom of the slope, the body was thoroughly battered, with a wide gash in the neck and strange marks on the face that did look a lot like bite or claw marks.

"We hope to learn more from the autopsy. Our coroners who attended the scene differed in opinion. One said he thought it did look like an animal attack but the other said definitely not. The body is with the forensic pathologist now," Waters said.

"What do you think?" Leblanc asked Katie.

"It doesn't look like a typical animal attack to me," she said slowly. "But I don't have a lot of experience in that regard."

"Me either," Leblanc admitted. In fact, during his time in Paris, the sum total of animal attack cases he'd handled had been one serious incident of dog bites. He hoped that a pathologist working in this area would have more experience in what to look for and how to differentiate.

Leblanc leaned forward, studying the image.

"He's got some wounds on his hands," Katie pointed out. "You can see blood through the gloves. He could have fought off an attacker carrying a bladed weapon."

Leblanc nodded. "But they could also be from an animal attack, or even from the fall."

He scanned the scene, searching for any signs that a human might have been here. For example, some footprints. There was nothing to be seen from the photos.

"We found a lot of blood frozen under the body, but we didn't find any discernible footprints at the scene, either animal or human," Waters explained.

The scene was cold and bleak and it had been well trampled by the investigators. He didn't think there was anything it could tell them. But he saw immediately that Katie thought differently

"There's always something more to find," she said, sounding optimistic. "Let's go further along the track and search. If there was a struggle, there might be evidence still hidden in the snow."

CHAPTER FIVE

Katie moved forward along the path. She knew that the detectives would have searched the scene and examined the area where the body had lain, but especially if they had believed it was an animal attack, they might not have looked searched in the detail that she thought was needed. Especially out in this bitter cold.

She didn't want to look where the body had been, but rather at the top of the slope, along the main pathway where she suspected the attack might have happened before the body had been pushed down. That was what she figured must have taken place if this had been a murder.

The wind was blowing, and it stung her face as it carried flecks of snow from the trees. Leblanc walked with her, looking down at the pathway.

"I don't see any heavy tracks that might have been made by an animal," Katie observed. Her partner frowned dubiously.

She knew Leblanc was leaning toward the theory that it had been an animal attack. She could see it clearly. But she didn't agree, believing that an animal would have left more visible spoor. If there was nothing to find, she reasoned, it surely meant tracks had been covered?

"You can't tell from photos," Leblanc argued. "And you can't tell from looking at the scene itself. The snow here has been churned up by the investigators. There are no clues about what exactly took place here."

"That's why we're looking for evidence," Katie told him patiently.

"So you're convinced there was a struggle, then," Leblanc said, with a trace of amusement.

"Yes I am, based on his hand injuries," she said.

"But he could have been defending himself against a wild animal, surely? Would you say you're going on hard evidence, or is it more instinct and gut feel?" he challenged. "The guy wasn't in good shape. He could have suffered a heart attack or stroke, especially while exerting himself in that cold."

"Instinct is always based on evidence. It's just subliminal, or not obvious enough for the conscious mind to take in," she said. She wasn't going to rise to his baiting.

"I'm just saying that if you are relying on instinct, then that's a little unscientific," he said.

"It's just practical experience. Something that you've learned and processed subconsciously," she said. "Once you've learned it, it becomes instinctive. There's a time and a place for everything," she said. "I'm happy to use the scientific method when it's appropriate. And I'm happy to use other methods too. Right now, that means carefully searching this snow for any evidence that might be hidden."

She cast him a look to say she'd had enough of his backchat. She thought he got the message, because he moved a few paces ahead, and began searching there.

She crouched down, moving aside some of the snow, just to see how deep it was and what might be hidden underneath. She picked up a few cubes of frozen snow, holding them on her hand so they wouldn't melt and drip. It brought back memories of the treasure hunts she and Josie used to create in the snow, and how they'd learned to follow the spoor of the passing wildlife, sometimes tracking them for miles.

Looking more carefully, and found a few flecks of congealed blood in the thinner sections.

She felt a thrill of excitement. That was a good sign that there had been a struggle in this spot and that the victim had at least tried to defend himself briefly. She marked the place where she'd found the blood, and then stood up.

Moving farther along, she found a patch of snow that was thinner, and she dug a little deeper, carefully moving aside the soft snow.

"There's something here," she said.

"I don't see anything," Leblanc said.

"There's a bit of blood here," she said. "So that would indicate a wider struggle, or else that the body was moved, and pushed down the slope."

"Okay. It is." Leblanc sounded reluctantly impressed.

Katie felt excited. She was sure this meant progress. There must be something left. Some detail, something small. A struggle scene was always a treasure trove for trace evidence.

Her hands moved carefully through the snow. It wasn't soft and loose but felt more compacted than it should. At some recent stage, people had moved through it.

"There can be bits of evidence hidden away in small corners," she said. "I'm sure we can find something. It's a good thing we got here as early as we did."

She felt determined to prove her point. For years after Josie's disappearance, she'd dreamed of finding a tiny clue, something that would provide answers. She'd had nightmares that the search parties had missed something important.

She was not going to give up now.

"It's just snow," Leblanc said. "That's why I don't understand what you're looking for."

"If there was a struggle, something might have been dropped or fallen, or come loose."

"I suppose you've done this before - searched for evidence in snow."

"I have," she said, tersely, deciding not to give details because she didn't want to mention her sister to him.

"You can't even tell if that blood is from an animal or human," he said.

That was true. But it was all they had so far. She cast around, examining the terrain. There was no sign of a struggle. There were no footprints. But she was certain that the tracks had been covered, and if so, then the signs of the struggle would have been, too.

She guessed the victim had not struggled for long. He'd tried briefly to defend himself and then died from that awful wound. Perhaps the killer had been too careful, and there was nothing to be found after all.

But then her fingers touched something hard and small within the snow.

Carefully, she picked it out and held it up.

"Look here," she said.

Leblanc's combative mood had simmered down, and he had resumed working quietly on his own. He swung around when she spoke, looking excited.

"What's that?"

"It's a scrap of leather."

Leblanc's head snapped up.

"I thought it might have been a piece of the attacker's clothing," Katie said. "But I'm not so sure now."

"You think it was from the struggle?"

"Yes. It was under a very thin layer of snow," she said.

"Let's see?" He scrunched toward her and squinted down at it.

"It's thick. That's not from clothing. More likely from a tool."

"From a stick? A handle of something? The grip of a knife?"

She felt a shiver of excitement. The scrap of leather was minuscule, but it was still something. She wondered if it was important.

"It could be part of a knife," Leblanc agreed.

"I'm going to bag this and take it back to the lab," she said. "It's no coincidence that it was right here, at the scene, and under a very thin layer of snow. It definitely couldn't have been there long or it would be more deeply covered."

She looked down at the piece of leather. She knew it would be a long, laborious process of examination, but she felt hopeful that there would be something there that could help them. It was the tiny details that made the difference.

Katie carefully put the scrap of leather into a plastic evidence bag and sealed it with a label. Then she slipped it into her pocket. For the first time, she felt they were getting somewhere. They had a clue that was real, not just a feeling.

Katie cast around once again but this time, her search didn't uncover anything. There was nothing else she could see except the dull, lifeless trees on the other side of the road. The branches were heavy with snow.

In this beautiful, remote area someone had attacked Banks. She was sure of it.

Perhaps the scrap of leather would guide their thinking, but for now she felt she was done here and there didn't seem to be anything else to find.

It was time to look into the evidence that the professionals could uncover - the secrets that the body itself would be hiding.

"Shall we go to the pathologist's office now?" she asked.

Leblanc nodded agreement.

"Let's go, he said.

CHAPTER SIX

The closest medical examiner's office to Diamond Ice Ranch was located an hour's drive away, in Billings, Montana. They drove there in one of the ranch's SUVs, identical to the one they had been transported in to view the scene.

As she pulled up outside the low, brick building set in a bleak, snow-covered parking lot, Katie was reminded all over again that at this ranch, no expense had been spared in ensuring the well-being of guests. It had been a luxury drive. The SUV's heater worked brilliantly and it felt comfortable and stable on the road.

She climbed out, reaching into her coat pocket for the important item of evidence that she'd brought along with her. She hoped that this leather scrap would provide a lead, or a link, to what they needed.

They hurried through the flurrying wind, and into the pathologist's offices.

The place was warm and quiet. They were met by a receptionist, who directed them to a narrow corridor with a view of a yard, where snow was whirling in the wind. They walked down the corridor and found the door they were looking for.

Katie knocked.

The door opened to reveal a man in his early fifties. He had short grey hair and a pleasant, welcoming manner. He was still gloved and gowned up, and Katie guessed he'd just finished working on the autopsy.

"Good afternoon," the pathologist said. "Please come in. So you're the police officers who are working the Banks case."

"That's right, said Katie. "Agent Winter and Detective Leblanc."

"Bob Deverell," the pathologist said.

Katie motioned to the evidence bag in her hand.

"I've brought something for you. I found it on the pathway, about two yards from where the body had fallen."

The pathologist held up the bag, scrutinizing the leather scrap inside. Then he nodded, and quickly disappeared through a side door. They heard him speaking in a low voice, and a moment later he was back.

"I've handed that to the forensic techs," he said. "Now, I guess you'd like to view the body and hear my insights so far?"

"Please," Katie said.

Deverell gestured to a cupboard.

"Your PPE is in there. Join me in the next room as soon as you're ready."

He opened the door at the back of the room and walked through.

Katie and Leblanc donned their outfits, putting on blue plastic aprons, gloves, head covers and masks. Katie looked at Leblanc, checking he was prepared. He nodded his readiness, and they stepped into the next room.

The autopsy room was bright and white, and looked more like an office than a morgue. It was a small, clinical room with a row of cupboards on one side, and brightly lit.

She breathed in the smell of the place. It always reminded her of her high school science lab, with a hint of chlorine and antiseptic, and a stronger presence of formaldehyde. With this still-fresh body, there was no trace of decay or putrefaction.

Deverell directed them toward a table, which was clean and contained a sheet-covered body. Then he stepped back.

"Here we are," he said.

Katie looked down, feeling a familiar lurch. The sheet was stained with blood, a side-effect from any autopsy.

Deverell drew it back and revealed the corpse on the table. Beside it were surgical instruments and bottles of chemicals.

She took a step forward and stared down at the body. She saw a waxen face, eyes closed, the lips a little parted. The face was pitted with small cuts and slices that looked deeper than they had done in the photos. The gash in the neck looked even uglier than the photos had portrayed.

Her stomach clenched as she imagined the scene playing out, and the moments of panic and pain that the victim must have felt.

"He was fully clothed, in cold weather outdoor clothing," Deverell said. "He was wearing a red parka, a fleece hat and fleece gloves. He had a pair of heavy boots on, and the snowshoes were still on his feet."

"What about the wounds on his hands? Would you say those are defensive wounds?" she asked, exchanging a glance with Leblanc.

"Yes, I would say so," he said. "There was a deep wound on his right hand, and a thin scratch on the right arm. As you know, he was killed by the injury to the neck. It's a deep wound and the bleeding was bound to be fatal, as it punctured the carotid artery in the neck. The other wounds on his face were most likely inflicted after death. They bled very little."

That was interesting, she thought. So Banks would probably have seen the killer before he struck. But perhaps he'd only realized at the last minute that this was a deadly confrontation. Hence the defensive wound as he tried, too little and too late, to protect himself.

"What is your opinion? Human or animal?" Leblanc said. Katie knew, with a sudden and unexpected flash of humor, that her opinionated partner wanted so badly to be right.

"The neck wound is sharp and clean, but there is some tearing in the flesh. It is my belief that this injury was caused by a knife with a serrated or twisted edge. Definitely an unusual weapon, but there's no sign of fur in the wounds at all, no dirt, no trace of claws, and nothing that stands out as a claw or tooth mark. But it's almost as if the killer wanted it to seem that way," he said thoughtfully.

"To mimic that an animal caused the wounds?"

"Exactly."

Katie looked at Leblanc who glanced back at her with a tinge of defiance in his gaze.

"Could he have had a heart attack, a stroke, anything like that?" Leblanc asked.

"There are still one or two tests we need to do, but on preliminary examination, it doesn't appear so," Deverell replied.

Leblanc sighed. Katie could see he was disappointed that his theory had been wrong and hers right. But she also knew from experience that he would move forward with the new theory as passionately as she was doing.

Katie took a closer look at the wound. She had never liked autopsies, but knew how important it was to take in every detail of the death.

She looked down at the dead man. Banks's body was cold, and the edges of the lips were starting to darken. His face was expressionless and his skin was waxy and grey.

"Was he a fit man?" she asked. "Could he have been injured in the fall?"

"No, he was rather overweight," the pathologist confirmed. "But there are no obvious strains or sprains or head trauma that we can find, to indicate that he would have been badly injured through the fall."

Katie nodded. As she'd thought, every aspect of the postmortem confirmed her theory of a human attack.

At that moment, the side door opened. A masked and gowned tech walked in.

"We've conducted some tests on the piece of leather you brought in," he said.

"What did you find?" Katie turned to him eagerly.

"We're not sure where it is from. There are no fingerprints discernible. However, there is a trace of blood on it."

Katie glanced at Leblanc, noticing his eyebrows were raised in surprise.

"Animal or human blood?" he asked.

"The blood is human," the tech said.

Katie looked back at the dead body. "Is there any way to test the blood type?" she asked.

"We'll do a DNA test on it next, to see if it is a match with the victim. If it isn't we'll keep it on the records, and with any luck, it can help us down the line."

"Great," Katie said, and Leblanc nodded in approval.

"I think that's all we need," he said.

Deverell showed them out, and they made their way back to Katie's car. They were both quiet as they drove away.

"What do you think?" Leblanc said.

"Banks's killer is clever," Katie said. "He's staged the scene to make it look like a predator attack. He knew Banks was walking in the woods, and he knew where he would be."

"So he lay in wait. He could have planned this for a while," Leblanc said.

"But why?" Katie thought aloud. "What made him attack?"

"Or her," Leblanc said, with a sideways glance at Katie. "Remember, his wife was in the chalet and didn't go with him on this outdoor jaunt, even though they'd done everything together on the rest of their vacation. And even though there are similarities with the Canadian case, that one could have been an animal attack, and this one a spousal murder."

"True," Katie nodded.

"We need to speak to the wife next," Leblanc decided.

"Yes. We need to confirm the timeline of where Banks went this morning, and who knew where he'd be. And we need to find out if Mrs.

Banks's movements were accounted for at the time," Katie decided. "If they weren't, then we already have a potential killer."

CHAPTER SEVEN

Leblanc was feeling thoughtful as they returned to the Diamond Ice Ranch. He'd been wrong about the marks being from an animal attack. The pathologist had confirmed they were made by an unusual blade.

However, that didn't mean the other body, found in Canada, was necessarily the same M.O. That one could simply have been a coincidental death. And if so, it meant they had to question Mrs. Banks very carefully. The spouse was always a suspect in a murder like this.

The good weather was holding, and the ranch's impressive frontage was bathed in late afternoon sun. He saw a few horses out in the pastures, eating piles of hay placed in the snow.

Katie parked outside the main building and they headed in. Immediately, one of the pretty receptionists hurried over to greet them. There were a couple of guests checking out, with their designer luggage piled high on one of the wheeled carriers. They didn't look happy. A porter was adding more wood to the log fire burning in the huge fireplace on the far side of the room.

"How can I help?" the receptionist asked with a stressed smile.

"We would like to interview Mrs. Banks," Katie said.

"I'm afraid Mrs. Banks is still in her room. She wasn't well this morning, and of course she's shattered after what's happened," the receptionist said.

"That's fine. If you could call through to the chalet and ask her if she is ready to be interviewed, we'll be there in five minutes, and can speak to her in her room," Leblanc insisted.

Nodding in understanding, the receptionist hurried behind the counter and got on the phone.

"She'll see you," she told them with a smile, replacing the receiver. "She's in chalet number three, which is one of the closer ones to the main building. It's down the path to the left."

"Thanks," Katie said.

Leblanc turned and walked out with her.

The wind was cold and brisk, but the pathway to the chalet had been swept free of blowing snow. The chalet itself was a large, sumptuous-looking, free-standing building that was constructed from wood and bricks. Katie tapped on the wooden front door and a moment later, a slender blonde woman opened it.

She was wearing a white dressing gown. Her face was pale and her eyes red-rimmed. She stared at them, blinking rapidly.

"I'm so sorry about your husband," Katie said. "Please accept our condolences. We are from the special task force, and we'd like to ask you some questions, if you feel up to it?"

"Yes - yes, I guess I do," Mrs. Banks said softly. "Please, come in."

Leblanc and Katie entered the chalet and looked around.

The chalet was a large, open-plan property with a contemporary, Scandinavian-style décor.

The walls were painted in clean, light colors and the expensive furniture looked as if it had been brought in from a high-end furniture shop. The place smelled of polished wood and fresh pine. A fire burned brightly in the fireplace.

Leblanc followed Katie inside, and they sat on one of the two plush settees in the lounge area. Leblanc noted that Mrs. Banks was petite and well groomed, with large eyes and high cheekbones. Her skin looked expensively cared for.

Looking closely at her, Leblanc saw that the blond, beautiful woman looked devastated. As a cop, he'd seen many distraught people act this way after losing a partner, from all walks of life. Sometimes it was genuine, but often it wasn't.

"Are you prepared to answer a few questions?" Katie asked.

"I'm willing to help, if I can," Mrs. Banks sighed.

"Thank you. Can you tell us why you and your husband came on this trip?" Katie asked.

"It was a spur-of-the-moment vacation. We usually go skiing around this time of year, but decided on the ranch vacation instead for something different. Friends of ours came here last year and enjoyed it," Mrs. Banks explained.

"Did you meet or interact with anyone else here on the ranch?" Katie asked.

"No. It was just us," Mrs. Banks said. "I didn't even know the name of the other guests. We kept ourselves to ourselves, like everyone else here seems to do."

"Up until now, you did the activities as a couple," Leblanc asked. "But this morning your husband went out on his own?"

"Yes. He said he wanted to go snowshoeing, but I decided not to go with him," Mrs. Banks said. "I had a migraine. I get them every so often. He went out after breakfast, while I slept in."

Leblanc knew he needed to confirm her alibi. She could have left the chalet and headed out after him.

"Do you know what time he left?" Leblanc said.

"Around eight, I guess."

"Was there anyone who saw you after that time?" Leblanc asked. "Or anyone who can confirm you were here in your room when your husband went out?"

The tears began to run down her cheeks.

"I didn't go out. I was lying in bed, waiting for the pain to pass. I didn't even know he was missing until the police came to the door and told me."

Leblanc frowned. This was sounding like Mrs. Banks had no alibi at all. But then she drew in a quick breath.

"Wait, I did have a few interactions with staff. I called the concierge at about half past eight and asked if they could bring me an ice pack to help with the pain. They delivered it to my room straight away. And then, it must have been about a half-hour after that, when the housekeeper knocked on the door, wanting to do up the room. "I told her that I wasn't ready to get up yet and that I would call her when I was."

Leblanc nodded, making a mental note to check this with housekeeping when they had finished the interview.

"Did you know where he was going?"

She shook her head.

"I had no idea. We'd walked, hiked, skied, snowshoed around the entire ranch over the past week. We both wanted to get into shape on this vacation. He was unfit and wanted to lose some weight, but he was finding that in the cold, he suffered from exertional asthma."

"Did that affect him on this vacation?"

"Yes, it meant we had to take things slowly when we went out. I had no idea which direction he was going in this morning, but he did tell me he'd be a couple of hours and that he wasn't going to rush. I'm still not sure where it happened. The police offered to take me out there but I didn't want to see it." She took a shaky breath.

Doing the math, Leblanc reckoned that timeframe didn't give her enough time to have gone out after him, because the murder scene was half an hour's walk away. She could have driven, though, if her car could have handled it.

"What car do you drive?" he asked, remembering that only a four-wheel drive could have gone out on those tracks.

She looked briefly confused.

"A Porsche and a Land Rover. But we don't have them here. We helicoptered in."

That confirmed to Leblanc that she could not have had the opportunity to follow her husband with the intention of murdering him.

"Do you think there was anything troubling your husband? Anything you noticed in the last few days that was out of the ordinary?" Katie asked gently.

Mrs. Banks gave a small shrug. "No. He was his normal self."

“Had you two been fighting or arguing recently? Any causes for conflict in your relationship?”

She stared at them, seeming genuinely puzzled. “Nothing like that at all. We’d been happily married nearly twenty years. Beyond the odd disagreement, we didn’t fight.”

"Did he seem worried about anything? Were there any negative interactions with any staff, or any guests?" Katie asked.

"No. Not that I can think of," Mrs. Banks said, shaking her head.

"Can you think of any reason why anyone would want to hurt your husband?" Katie said.

She shook her head. "No. I just don't understand."

Katie nodded.

"Thank you so much for your time, and for answering the questions. I know it can't have been easy for you."

She got up and Leblanc followed her out, leaving the bereaved wife to gather herself after the interview.

They walked slowly and thoughtfully back to the lodge. Leblanc thought that, between them, they had ruled out any obvious motives for the killing.

But the questioning had given him an important insight.

"The Banks were out and about every day as a couple," he mused, staring down at the perfectly swept paving.

"Yes, they were," Katie said, and Leblanc realized she, too, was thinking along the same lines.

"But he was murdered when he went out on his own. That's very convenient, don't you think?"

"I do," she agreed. "It means that the killer, whoever he or she was, must have been on site at the time. And if this is a true serial killer, selecting his victims on the basis of being vulnerable to him, he might have been watching out for a guest heading into the grounds alone."

Leblanc shivered.

Undoubtedly, the killer was familiar with the ranch, and had been waiting to identify a victim. And that meant that the staff were now the next suspects in this crime.

CHAPTER EIGHT

He liked to be known as M, even though it had little connection with his real name.

M was the middle letter of the alphabet which he liked because it felt balanced, it felt like he was joining two sides together. It was the middle ground. The no-man's land between poverty and wealth, the haves and the have-nots.

He liked to feel that he bridged that gap every time he killed.

M stood for Murder, but it also stood for Motive.

M smiled to himself as he washed the twisted steel blade carefully in the small sink at the back of his hideaway.

He was glad that he lived here all by himself in this remote place. He was glad that he didn't have to hide his true self where others could see him.

He felt grateful he had this space to shelter him. It was a refuge. Not just from the world, but from the forces of nature too. He liked the power of this place.

The blade was so sharp that he had to be careful. It was as sharp as the jagged teeth and claws of a predator. He'd forged it himself; he had a little knowledge of steelwork and was good with his hands. Not enough to be an expert by any means, but enough rudimentary knowledge to have created this unique, solid blade. It was all the more effective for being so crude.

The blade would serve a purpose again. Finally, it was being used for the reasons he had made it. Despite the fact that he had made sure no one else saw him in the act, he felt pride in how sharp and durable it was.

M was confident that no one would be able to connect him to the murder or the dead man. The frozen body was out of sight and out of mind now.

M enjoyed washing the knife because he liked being a meticulous man. He smiled as he washed the blade, which had now been used twice and needed a thorough clean.

Meticulous. That was another good word for him, despite what they'd said about him and how unfair they'd been. He was showing them his true character now.

His smile was warm as it reflected in the polished steel.

He took a cloth, wrapped it around the knife handle, then laid the knife on a newspaper to dry. Then he gave a small shudder, part thrill, part dread.

He remembered the expression of surprise that had replaced the arrogance on that rich guy's face, moments before he died. Surprise and fear, too late to save him.

M felt his heart quicken in his chest.

The man's eyes had been filled with fear, just before he'd left this world. A terror that had spread quickly, as his million-dollar heart gave out, a victim of a fifty-dollar knife.

M smiled, feeling pleased that a humble, crudely crafted blade could be such an equalizer. He liked to think that the knife was a force of nature, like a tornado or a lightning strike. Unstoppable, powerful.

And then he remembered the moment of the kill itself. He had got the blade into the guy in one swift motion. The man had barely had time to register it. The blade had gone in cleanly and deeply, and then he had pulled it out as quickly, letting the weight of the body drag it out of the snow, away from the tracks of the other guests and staff.

The tracks were the only danger. It was important to make sure he covered his footprints well enough that they couldn't be identified or followed. But basic wilderness skills and the help of a tree branch did the job until he was far enough from the scene.

He'd always told himself that he only killed the deserving ones. He only killed the people who deserved it. But the truth was, he enjoyed it. He enjoyed the hunt, the kill and the thrill of the moment when they knew they were dying.

When their money meant nothing.

Money. Another M word to ponder over.

M had been born in the depths of despair.

His father had been a man with a violent temper who used to beat him and his mother before she'd left him for an alcoholic.

He'd struggled to make his way in the world, and the disdain and prejudice that others had shown, had always cut him deep.

He had always been repelled by the arrogance the wealthy patrons at these ranches showed. At first, he'd wanted their life, and been fascinated by it. What he would do with that money! But then he'd seen the way they looked down on other people, flushed with the certainty that they were invulnerable, untouchable.

They didn't have to worry about their money. They could dress in their designer-label clothes, live in their huge houses with their heated swimming pools and have their money managed by experts.

How important their lives were, and how little they cared about his own.

Now that he had a purpose, he could see the injustice.

He felt exhilarated that finally, after years of being a victim, struggling and failing and being looked down on, his resolve had crystallized and he had decided to change things. Now, he had a role to play, a mission to fulfill. He'd discovered that the wealthy could be as vulnerable as anyone else. They could be as easy to kill as any other human.

Step by step, he was going to correct the unfairness and the imbalance of it all.

Abruptly, he stood up. He felt energized after the kill. Adrenaline was still surging. He didn't want to rest now.

Not when there were more targets out there, people on their own, confident and arrogant as they strode along, believing their wealth could protect them from any wrong in the world and allow them to behave as they pleased.

His home was close to the border, nestled on the USA side. In the big, wild, poorly policed expanse, it was easy to criss-cross that imaginary line, and access ranches on both sides.

He put on his insulated parka and thick snow boots with their chunky tread. He zipped his knife into his pocket, then left the cottage, closing the door quietly behind him.

As he walked through the snow towards his truck, he felt the strength of the knife inside his pocket, like a talisman of power, a talisman of change.

Change.

He liked the word. He liked the idea that something as simple as a knife could change things.

He smiled and climbed into his truck, turned the key and drove away into the heavy snowfall of the mountains.

He had more targets to find. And he had a place to do it.

He'd been inside Caribou Wilderness Resort, which nestled just north of the border. He knew it well. And he'd done a recce of the wider area a few days ago, where he'd been almost run off the road to it by the demented, entitled drivers speeding there in their bulky SUVs.

He'd seen the vast parking lot filled with the SUVs and sports cars of the trust fund babies and the rich retirees, that he remembered from the last time he'd set foot inside the grounds. Soon, that would change. There wouldn't be many people wanting to go there once he'd done his work.

M smiled, looking at himself in the mirror, briefly puzzled by how normal and ordinary he looked, despite his unusual and in fact, unique thoughts and actions.

He was meticulous, but he was also invisible.

No one would ever suspect him.

M picked up his knife and put it carefully in the sheath on his belt. Then he climbed into his car and drove out, heading for the curling, narrow road that led up to Caribou Wilderness Resort,.

In the glare of the low afternoon sun, he drove slowly, carefully.

He felt himself getting excited again as he thought of what lay ahead and how he would plan. His heart was beating faster and his breathing was shallow and fast.

Soon, it would be time.

CHAPTER NINE

"The staff might either be involved in some way, or know more about this," Katie said to Leblanc, as they entered the main building of Diamond Ice Ranch. Ideas were spinning through her head. Someone recently fired could have decided on payback. Or perhaps an employee had had an issue with that particular guest. Those were her first thoughts. A normal person would never dream of going as far as murder, but they were not in the territory of normal behavior here. They were far beyond that, in the realm of those shadowy individuals who were true psychopaths.

She headed straight up to the friendly receptionist who'd greeted them the last time.

"How many staff does this ranch employ?" she asked.

"Quite a number," the receptionist said, giving Katie that automatic smile again as she turned to the computer. "We have the housekeeping staff, the concierge, the management, the groundsmen, ranch admin. The chefs and kitchen staff. And then the outdoor staff. The ski instructors, the shooting instructors, the horse grooms and stable assistants and riding instructors. All in all, about forty people. Then we're also a working ranch, and have a separate team of about five cowboys and managers who deal with our cattle, but they don't come into contact with guests at all."

That was a lot to interview, Katie thought, reminded once again of exactly what a big business this ranch was and how much political clout the industry carried.

"Do you know of anyone in the ranch who had issues with Mr. Banks? Perhaps he complained about somebody or had an argument with a member of staff?"

She shook her head.

"Our staff are trained to be polite but we also have a policy that any difficult guests are reported to the management and flagged, so that we make sure to be very careful around them. Mr. Banks was not a difficult guest and had not been flagged," she said.

Katie nodded.

She felt disappointed that there was no clear direction to go on here. No conflict or unpleasantness that might have triggered the need for revenge. But now, it was time to find out if the staff had seen anything that could be helpful.

"I'd like to speak to the people who were working outdoors, or in that area, at around the time Mr. Banks set out for his walk," she said. "They might have seen something, or noticed someone following him. Could you call them into the lounge and we can ask a few questions?"

"Sure," the receptionist said, pressing keys on her phone and turning to her computerized list.

*

Ten minutes later, a group of people had gathered in the lounge. Clustered near the fireplace, Katie thought they looked reluctant and nervous. They were dressed in heavy jackets and boots and had the lean, wiry bodies of people who worked outdoors in substantial cold and did large amounts of exercise.

She surveyed the group, and her gaze rested on a tall man with neatly cut brown hair and worried blue eyes, who seemed particularly uneasy and uncomfortable to be there, shifting his feet and looking at the door.

"Would you come through with me, please?" she said to him. Looking around, Katie saw a door leading into a plush library. "Shall we speak in here?"

She led the way inside, seeing that Leblanc was doing the same on the opposite side of the large room.

"Were you working outdoors this morning?" she asked.

The man nodded, frowning anxiously. "I was sweeping the paths between the chalets, going out to the riding trails and hiking routes."

"Did you see Mr. Banks leave? The time would have been at around eight."

"Yes, I think I saw him head out. Wearing a red parka? I think he was holding snowshoes."

“Did you interact with him at all? Or had you interacted with him previously?”

He shook his head. “I was too far away to greet him. I noticed him leave, because he was walking a path I'd recently swept. I remember being glad about that, because the guests sometimes complain if the paths aren't freshly done when they go out. I'd seen him a couple of times over the past few days but never spoken to him. We don't shout to guests. Only greet if they are within normal speaking distance."

"Did you see anyone else around?" Katie asked.

"Yes. There was a chef, delivering room service to guests."

"Did anyone follow him out to the trails, that you saw?"

The man frowned. "No. I didn't see anyone else. But I was focused on what I was doing. We are trained that we must greet the guests but we mustn't stare at them or start up a conversation. They are very wealthy people, and we have to respect their privacy. So I keep to myself. We all do. You don't want to mess up, working here," he mumbled.

Katie looked at him, feeling sympathy, because she suspected his uneasy demeanor was more from nervousness than any guilt. It must be hard work, doing what he did in this weather with the temperature so cold. It was even harder when catering for a high-end clientele, who would be either 'discerning' or 'picky, depending on which side of the spectrum you looked.

"What time did you finish your shift?"

"Twelve o'clock, exactly. I took an hour's lunch break, and then went out to the main driveway in the afternoon."

"When you were sweeping the paths, did you notice anyone at all go out that way soon after Mr. Banks? Or anyone come back from that route?"

"No, ma'am. I'm sorry. I do think I would have noticed if anyone else had gone from the chalets," he explained. "But the ranch is huge, and the wranglers looking after the cattle sometimes use those paths, too. We've even had guests from other ranches getting lost on long mountain bike rides or horse rides, and finding their way down to us."

"Thanks for explaining that. I won't need anything further from you," she said. His words reinforced that the sheer size of these ranches made it all too easy for people to come and go, and to disappear in the tracts of wilderness and forest.

But she wasn't going to give up just yet, and was going to ask a few more people, in case someone had noticed a staff member sneaking out onto the trails.

The man left and Katie turned to the next person, a woman dressed in a very warm, heavy jacket and knee-high boots.

"What were you doing outside this morning?" she asked the woman.

"I was cleaning snow off the guests' cars," she said.

"And did you see anyone arriving, or heading out to the trails?"

"Yes. There was a chef delivering breakfast sets to the guest rooms. I noticed him walk from the chalets, back to the kitchen, because he greeted me and called out good morning."

"Did you see Mr. Banks leave at all? Wearing a red parka?"

She looked conflicted.

"No, ma'am, I am really sorry but I didn't see him. I have to be careful working on the guests' cars. I don't have time to look around when I'm cleaning and polishing the cars."

"Do you know of anyone who had a grudge against the guests, or who was angry at them?

"No. I've been here a year, and I genuinely can't think of anyone who would be that angry. I mean, some of the guests have a temper. But to do that? I just can't believe it," she said sadly.

"Thank you," Katie said. She felt thoughtful that the woman had pointed out the element of anger. Perhaps that was something she needed to keep in mind.

The woman left and Katie turned to her next witness.

He was a cowboy in a black jacket and suede chaps.

"Were you out on the trails in the morning?" Katie asked him.

"Yes, ma'am. I was out on the trails with two guests. We left at eight, for a two-hour ride."

"Did you see Mr. Banks this morning?"

"I did. I saw a man in a red parka setting out on the trail at the same time we left."

"Did anyone follow Mr. Banks?"

"No, ma'am. I don't recall seeing anyone at all, but we were on a fast ride, and we were out of sight of the chalets very soon."

"Do you know if anyone working here had an issue with Mr. Banks, or with any of the guests? Was anyone angry or resentful?"

The man thought hard.

"No, I can't say I noticed anything like that. We all do our jobs, ma'am, and we're lucky to have them. This ranch pays better than the average and there are bonuses in the busy season," he added solemnly.

Katie nodded.

"Thank you," she said.

She mulled over what she had learned.

The staff were busy, and were trained not to stare at guests. And, due to the vastness of the ranch, it would be very easy for the killer to have simply avoided anywhere that people were likely to be, or to have walked out of sight if someone approached. Unfortunately, for a serial killer, this provided a perfect environment to strike undetected.

She felt frustrated that with so many staff, nobody had seen or heard anything helpful. It was a dead end, and one they didn't need.

At that moment, Katie's phone rang. She picked it up.

"It's Deverell from the forensics lab, Agent Winter," a man's voice said.

Katie felt hope flare inside her. Had he found evidence that might provide a lead?

"We've analyzed the blood trace from the leather scrap you brought in."

"What have you found?"

"It wasn't a match with the victim. However, we then decided to see if there was any link between this and the related case. So we contacted the pathology lab that dealt with the Canadian victim."

Katie's eyebrows raised. That had been good thinking.

"Was there any match?" she asked.

"Yes. There was a match. The blood on the leather scrap you found is an exact DNA match with the blood of the victim from the Maple Creek ranch. So without a doubt, these two killings are linked."

Katie felt a surge of adrenaline.

This was a massively important discovery and it widened the scope of the investigation. But at the same time, it made the situation vastly more dangerous. No longer were they only looking at the staff and guests of Diamond Ice ranch. A killer was moving around in the area. And it was a real possibility that two kills might soon become three.

With any luck, one of the staff here would have noticed something helpful. These interviews would take the rest of the day to complete. But even if there was no information to be gained, they now had an important new direction to follow.

First thing tomorrow, Katie decided they should go to Maple Ranch to discover more about where, and how, this murdering spree had begun.

CHAPTER TEN

When Katie and Leblanc arrived in Maple Creek the following morning, to meet with the RCMP detectives who had handled this murder case, the sun was just starting to rise. She felt hopeful about what they might discover on this side of the border.

As they arrived in town, Katie noted that it was a three-hour drive between Diamond Ice ranch and this small town, which was just north of Maple Ranch where the murder had occurred. A three hour drive was not far at all in this vast region, and it meant that the killer could easily have commuted between the murder sites by car or even snowmobile.

They'd left in the dark, departing at five-thirty a.m. after what Katie had to admit was a very comfortable night's sleep. The ranch, grateful for the cross-border task force's help, had put them up in two luxury chalets, with room service meals included.

Katie was glad that she'd had a good night's rest because she had a feeling this was going to be a tough and long day.

Their first stop was the small RCMP office in Maple Street. There, Katie hoped, they would find out what they needed about the first victim, Elaine Malanchuk. They parked outside the building and walked in. A police detective immediately hurried over to them.

"Agent Winter?" he asked.

"Yes," Katie said.

"I'm Detective Davidson, Maple Creek RCMP. I spoke to you yesterday evening, when you called," he said.

"We appreciate you meeting with us first thing," Katie assured him.

"I've got the case file in the back office, so you can take a look before we head to the site," the detective said.

They walked into the station.

Katie looked around, noticing the posters on the wall. They were old posters, and seemed to have been put up for the sake of tradition rather than anything else. She guessed that in this small town, violent crime was a shocking rarity.

He led them to a small office and invited them to take a seat.

As Katie paged through the printed information, Davidson filled them in.

"We were called out on the search after Elaine Malanchuk failed to arrive back at the ranch after going out on a hike. Because the area is so vast, we searched for two days and eventually a police helicopter spotted her body, which had fallen down a steep embankment."

"This was how long after she had left the ranch?" Leblanc asked.

"She was seen leaving the ranch at around nine in the morning, and her husband reported her missing at lunch time. He'd been out the whole morning with an ice fishing group," Davidson explained. "The search began in the afternoon. We resumed it the next day, but had to bring the helicopter back as there were very high winds and an unseasonal heavy rainfall. The helicopter went out again the day after that, and spotted her at around eleven in the morning."

"And you initially thought it was the fall that killed her, and the injury was caused by a wild animal?" Leblanc asked.

Davidson nodded.

"Her body fell into a sheltered ravine, near the woods. It was partially decomposed thanks to the brief thaw, and there was evidence of scavenging. Also, there was considerable damage to her skull and face from the fall. Because of all those factors, the pathologist was unable to confirm exactly what had caused the main injury to her throat."

Katie glanced over the information about the victim. Elaine Malanchuk was forty-three years old. Her ID photo showed a stylish woman, with expensive-looking blonde hair and top of the range hiking clothing.

"We'll need a copy of the crime scene photos," Leblanc said.

"They are available. You can view them on the screen here. Also, I can email them to you."

Katie studied the various photos. The terrain looked brutal. There was a series of steep, rocky outcroppings and heavy forest.

The woman was lying on her back, and had on new-looking hiking boots and taupe trousers.

Nodding slowly, Katie saw that the body had been there for some time before being found. The woman's head was turned to one side, and her face bore the same deep pock marks that Banks's had done. But in addition it showed genuine signs of animal scavenging. One eye was missing, although some tissue around it remained. Her right cheekbone looked like it had been chewed away.

She couldn't blame the police for coming to this conclusion, and was just grateful that the two cases had been linked so soon.

"Shall we take a drive to the ranch? It's twenty minutes from here," Davidson suggested.

They walked out to his car and climbed inside. He set off, and while they drove, Katie decided to question him further about the Malanchuks.

"Did Elaine work? And her husband?" she asked.

"She didn't work. Her husband owns several large manufacturing businesses in Houston. They traveled frequently I believe, and vacationed several times a year. He's devastated. As he was out all morning with a group, we cleared him immediately but asked him to stay one more night in case we had any further questions. He flew home the next day."

"Did you ask him if there were any problems with any staff at the ranch? Did he have any run-ins with anyone? Did he notice anyone who might have been watching him?" Katie asked, following up on this theory.

Davidson shook his head.

"We did ask those questions, but he said he noticed nothing out of the ordinary. They'd only been there two days when this happened. The previous day they had gone skiing together." Davidson made a grim face. "The ranch owners have been running the place for twenty years and they have never had any serious problems beforehand. Nothing like this has ever happened."

Katie saw that the ranch was ahead. It looked majestic, framed by soaring, snow-covered, craggy hills with tracts of rolling forest.

From the imposing gateway, she immediately saw this was a high-end place catering for wealthy guests.

Katie was interested to see that a security guard was standing at the gate, warmly wrapped and stamping his feet in the snowy cold.

"Is this guard a recent addition?" she asked.

"Yes," Davidson replied.

He stopped at the gate and showed his badge. The guard waved them through.

They drove up the tree-lined driveway to the main building and parked outside. The lodge looked huge. It was a sprawling wooden building framed by tall pine trees. In this cloudy morning, lights glowed from the windows.

Davidson got out and escorted them to the main entrance, where they were immediately greeted by the manager. Dressed in a gray parka, the harassed man looked to have been waiting for them, clearly alerted by the guard.

"I'm Owen Grant," the man said. "I'm the manager of Maple Ranch. Please, tell me what you need. We've just heard that it has been confirmed as a murder and we're all devastated it has happened, and seriously worried about it affecting the safety of future guests."

"This is Agent Winter, and Detective Leblanc from the cross-border task force," Davidson introduced them.

"Please, can you show us where Elaine Malanchuk died?" Katie asked.

"Sure. Let's go there straight away. It's a remote area so we'll need to go via snowmobile. It's very cold out, so you might want to put on an extra jacket, or a full suit."

Grant walked purposefully out of the lodge, to a large garage around the corner.

Inside, Katie saw there were several clothing racks and sets of snowmobiles. She accepted a thick jacket and pulled it on.

They climbed on the snowmobiles and Davidson led the way out of the hotel.

The snowmobile's roar was deafening as they sped across the open fields. Katie saw a plume of snow whirling up from where each tire landed.

The ride was fast, and Katie barely had time to take in the scenery, while concentrating on following Davidson, before he showed. They had arrived at the spot where Elaine's body had fallen. Davidson climbed off his machine and they stopped behind him.

The area was very remote. It was craggy and steep, just as the photos had shown, and thickly forested.

"It's a pretty isolated area," Davidson said, as he trudged along the narrow path to the big tree ahead that Katie recognized from the photographs.

"Did you find any footprints or other evidence of anyone else being here?" Leblanc asked.

Davidson shook his head. "It's unfortunate that so much time had passed. She headed out while there was a light snowfall so nobody knew which way she'd gone. Her tracks were already covered. Then the rain turned everything to mud for a day. Her phone was with her, but it broke in the fall, so we couldn't track the signal."

Katie looked down into the gorge. This was the area where Elaine's body had fallen from. The fall was approximately twenty feet down. It was overgrown and sheltered in the ravine.

"It really is miles from anywhere," she said.

This was deep in the ranch and nowhere near a road. Only the rustle of branches and the call of birds disturbed the silence.

Coming to this site had shown her that the killer must have a good knowledge of the layout of the local ranches, and that he - or she - must be familiar with the wilderness.

"I'm thinking we need to get back to the office now, and do some research. I want to look into what these ranches have in common, and see if we can identify a reason for why they were targeted," she said.

She had a new idea she was keen to pursue. Being just a few hours' drive apart, these ranches might well have had service providers or even employees in common. Any recent changes in those might mean someone felt unfairly treated, and had decided to damage both these businesses in a revenge move.

CHAPTER ELEVEN

"Well, c'mon guys, what's keeping you?" Staring back through his expensive sunglasses, Justin Gray regarded his fellow hikers impatiently.

He was part of the group of six guests from the luxury lodge who'd all chosen this challenging route on the cold but sunny morning, and all except him were struggling. Including his girlfriend, Patti. She was trailing at the back of the group because she was soft and unfit. The others were all taking strain because they were old and fat.

Not everyone owned a group of Crossfit franchises and could spend two hours a day in the gym, Justin thought disdainfully. People should take care of themselves. He might only be thirty, but he planned to look just as good when he was fifty. Unlike that balding guy, puffing along next to Patti.

"Hey, Patti!" He yelled at his girlfriend.

"She's doing her best," the balding guy said. There wasn't much humor in his tone. Justin thought he was about to lose it and would have lost it by now, except he hadn't had enough breath.

"I'm just trying to help her out," Justin said innocently.

The truth was he was becoming impatient with Patti. She was a pretty face, but she didn't give him enough attention, and he was starting to see her as a liability. After this vacation, he thought it would be time to move on.

"We'll have to turn around soon," said the old hiker.

"There's a pathway back to the main hotel a little further on," his pudgy and equally unfit wife said.

"You going to go for it?" Justin leaped from foot to foot, showing off his superior fitness as he waited for them to straggle up to where he stood. He hoped they were impressed. In truth, his legs were also aching from the climb although he'd never have admitted to it. It was a lot different out here in the snow, than it was in the gym. But he had his image to maintain and was going to do it, whatever it took.

"I don't think I can do another hill," the old guy at the front said. Maybe he and his wife were battling because they were older, but maybe they just had too much fat on them.

"Let me help you, Mrs. Porter." Patti had caught up and was offering to give the wife an arm.

"There's a break in the trees ahead," the balding guy announced. "That must be where the path goes."

"I think I'm going to call it a day," the old man said.

"Sure you want to?" Justin asked. "If you do, my girlfriend and I will go on alone."

They were all trying to catch their breath. He saw them glancing in the direction of the downward trail. They weren't going to tackle the mountain.

It was all about mind over matter. Something these fools would never realize, and now it was too late. Justin smirked inwardly, knowing he'd never be like them.

Justin was about to call Patti when he noticed she was putting on a good show, pretending she was trying to walk on a hurt ankle.

"What's wrong?" Justin jogged back to her.

"I think I twisted my ankle helping Mrs. Porter over that rocky outcrop. It hurts to walk," she said.

He flashed a superior smile. "You'd better go back with the others, then."

He'd done his best to prepare her for this trip, but she hadn't strengthened herself enough and taken enough classes. Now she was paying the price. He'd tried to warn her but she hadn't listened.

"I'll see you later, baby. Y'all know the way, right?" he asked.

Justin watched them go, feeling suddenly bad that she really was limping. A thought briefly occurred to him that if he'd been a truly caring person, he would have gone back with her and helped her down the steep hill.

He felt a moment's guilt, but brushed it off. If she'd really cared for him, she would have gotten herself fitter. That worked both ways, right?

Justin set off up the winding trail at a run, hoping that the others would see how fast he was going as he sped ahead.

The trail wound up the mountain through trees. Glancing left, he could see the sprawling buildings of the hotel far below.

He hoped they were enjoying seeing what he could really do. He wasn't in the mood for company anyway. Not when he was pushing himself to the limits on this uphill sprint.

The path was wide for a few hundred feet, then the land fell sharply away on one side and narrowed.

Justin picked up the pace and ran. The trees closed in on him. He was getting warm now, his breath coming in harsh gasps as he tried to increase his speed. Pulling off his woolen hat, he felt the wind in his hair as he pounded ahead. The breeze from the mountain was icy and refreshing. The undergrowth nearby in the pine forest was rustling. He could barely hear it above the sound of his breathing.

His legs were starting to burn seriously now. He didn't know how long he could keep this pace up. It wasn't only the punishing uphill, it was also the elevation. The air was thinner up here. His studios were at sea level. Despite himself, he dropped to a walk. Quickly, hoping nobody had seen, he pulled out his phone and took a selfie. That was an acceptable reason for a breather, right?

He took several while he caught his breath, making sure his handsome face looked just so, framed by the forest and mountains, his dark eyes narrowed. He thought of the hashtags he might use.

#FittestOfAll, #LastManStanding #CatchMeIfYouCan

He wanted to post it immediately, to rub it in for Patti, but saw to his annoyance that there was no signal up here.

Justin slipped the phone into his pocket. He was ready for the final ascent.

He set off again, deciding not to run this time. That sprint had taken it out of him. His legs were actually quivering now.

He proceeded at the fastest possible walk, checking the time. Despite his tiredness, he wanted to get up there quicker than anyone else would do.

And then, ahead of him, he heard the scrunch-scrunch of footsteps, coming down toward him through the woods. He could have sworn he was the only person hiking up here and felt briefly miffed that someone else had been to the top and was already on the way back. Maybe it was just a caretaker or groundsman who'd been out clearing the track, he thought hopefully.

In fact, the man who appeared through the trees, in a dull brown coat, did look like an employee of some kind. A gray man, Justin thought, noting the stoop of his shoulders and the bow of his head. The guy was probably his age, but you could see he was of no importance. Definitely a caretaker who'd probably been up here since early in the morning, preparing the trail for fast, fit guys like himself.

"Scuse me, dude, I need to pass," Justin barked at him, because the guy was in his way.

The man didn't seem to fully understand, but he moved aside.

"I'm sorry," he mumbled.

He gestured for Justin to pass, shuffling out of the way.

Justin strode forward, brisk and confident.

And then, when he was only a few yards away from the guy, disaster struck. Cramp lanced through his left quad, the pain searing.

Justin gasped, stumbling, almost losing his footing as he staggered forward, doubling over with pain. He could barely walk on the leg at all. What an embarrassment. Now this dude probably thought he was as soft and weak as the group he'd left behind.

But, as he lurched up the slope, he noticed something odd about the guy. The man was staring at him. He didn't look like a nobody anymore. There was a strange, predatory air about him as he regarded Justin intensely.

"Who are you looking at?" Justin gasped with irritation. Was this guy mocking or belittling him? He wasn't going to be disparaged by some random stranger just because he had a cramp, even if the guy was a bit taller and broader than he'd first supposed him to be.

He struggled past, preoccupied with the pain as he reached the other man. He wasn't going to look at him. This was too shameful.

But as he passed, the guy grabbed him, so suddenly and violently that Justin gasped.

He caught the guy's arm, trying to push it off, but the hand that held him was strong. It gripped his arm like a vise.

"What are you doing?" he exclaimed. His heart was pounding as a flood of fear surged. He should deck this guy, but how could he when his left leg was collapsing under him, and couldn't bear any weight?

And then, with a jolt of raw terror, he saw the weird, twisted knife the man held in his other hand. He was grasping its leather-wrapped handle tightly.

Justin had only the briefest view of its sharp, serrated blade before it flashed down toward him.

CHAPTER TWELVE

Maple Ranch was as eager to get the crimes solved as Diamond Ice had been, and Leblanc was impressed that they immediately made one of their two conference rooms available for him and Katie to work.

"This way. It's in here." Owen Craig, the ranch manager, ushered them into the room. It was a cozy space, with a large wooden table and eight leather-upholstered chairs. The room was warm and comfortable, and smelled of fresh coffee. There were plugs and connection points throughout the room, and a large white screen at one end. The walls were hung with historic photos of the ranch.

Katie took off her coat and sat down in one of the plush chairs. She took the folders of documents out of her bag while Leblanc set up his laptop.

"I feel like we're racing against time here," she muttered, and Leblanc nodded agreement.

"What can I get you?" Owen reappeared at the door, holding a tray of drinks and snacks which he placed on the table. "I'm sure you must be hungry. Here's some refreshments."

Leblanc glanced at Katie.

"Employee and service provider records will be helpful," he said. "We're going to collate all of them from the two ranches affected so far, and see if there are any staff or contractors common to both. In particular, we'd like to know about anyone who left on bad terms."

Owen nodded solemnly.

"I'll get them for you," he promised. "And I'll make sure we don't leave anything out."

"Thanks," said Leblanc. He opened his laptop and sat down opposite Katie, who was now on the phone to Diamond Ice.

"I'm investigating the case, and looking for your employee records and the contractors you've used," she said to the receptionist. "We need them urgently, going back a few months. In particular, anyone who was fired or whose services were terminated. Perhaps you could highlight those for us?"

She disconnected.

"They're sending now," she said. “I feel this is going to be important for us, and these records are by far the most likely place where we’ll find this killer.”

Leblanc felt encouraged that they could move fast on this.

"We can set up a search for records shared between the two ranches, and work out any connections. I'm guessing most of the service providers at both places will be locals," he said. "You’d need specialist knowledge to work in this area, and to have a local operations base."

Katie nodded. "Whoever this person is, they clearly do have knowledge of the local area and are able to move around easily."

At that moment, Owen rushed back in with printed sheaves of paper.

"Here are the two sets of records," he said. "We fired a couple of people in the past three months, and I have highlighted those. But far more of them quit. It's very hard work here. Not everyone can do it. We’ve had very few changes in our service providers, but again, I’ve highlighted those, with reasons where we have them."

Leblanc started working on the service providers for the past three months, while Katie took a look at the staff records.

Leblanc was impressed by the way she worked, so efficiently, like she had the whole story right in front of her. She was making notes on a pad as she read.

Her computer pinged.

"The lists from Diamond Ice Ranch are here," she said. "Probably easier to print them."

Leblanc hooked up to the printer in the corner of the room and soon they had the two sets of information in front of them.

“We need to look at the bigger picture,” Katie said. “These two ranches could have been targeted by a disgruntled former employee or service provider, who has turned into a serial killer in the last few months. He's going to be someone who might fit in and look normal, but who has been harboring a serious grudge against his employers. A normal person feeling that way might try something minor. Theft, petty arson, defaming the ranch on social media. But a psychopathic person will be triggered to kill, and sometimes it might only take the first kill for the chain of events to be set in motion. Then the inhibition to kill has been broken," she explained seriously.

So, who had left - quit or fired or their services no longer needed - from both establishments? That was the key question, and the place where Leblanc knew they urgently need to focus.

He began going through the pages of material, checking and crosschecking every entry. This type of work always made him feel anxious as it would be so easy to miss something critical just through human error.

Immediately, he saw there was a big difference between Diamond Ice Ranch and Maple Ranch. While Diamond Ice had a low staff turnover, Maple Ranch was the opposite. Katie agreed, as she frowned down at the page.

"This ranch does have a high staff turnover," Katie said. "I don't know if you're seeing this on your side, but between seasonal workers taken on at peak times, and people who quit, there's a lot of change here. A lot of opportunity for someone to be discontented. This might be the luxury market but to me, it doesn't feel like a stable industry."

Leblanc agreed. "I am seeing it," he said. "They have switched service providers frequently and often just based on a cheaper price."

There were a lot of flash points in the records. A lot of opportunities where staff or businesses might have left feeling angry and hard done by. With so many changes, working through them was a challenging task.

But now what they needed to look for was the businesses, or workers, that both ranches had fired or stopped using.

*

Fifteen minutes later, Leblanc looked up from his pages.

"I think I've got something," he said.

Katie scooted around to his side of the table, looking motivated.

Leblanc double checked the list, ensuring that the individual he had pinpointed had worked at both ranches.

"It's a guy called Richard Lang, who provided equestrian supplements and feeds on behalf of a company called Equest Pro. I've noted here that both places stopped using him. Diamond Ice noted that he was rude to their staff and to their guests and they couldn't have him on the premises any longer. They kept using Equest Pro but requested that a different agent call on them."

"Go on?" Katie said.

“I see here he actually got into a fist fight with the stable manager at Maple Ranch and they stopped using Equest Pro entirely based on that. I’ve looked on the company’s records online and he no longer seems to be working for them, so that must have led to him being fired.”

“How long ago was this?”

“It looks like this came to a head at both places during the fall. So that would be about three months ago?”

He looked at Katie, and saw the same excitement in her eyes.

"He's a strong common denominator. I'm sure of it," Leblanc said, thinking out loud. "He got into trouble with both ranches, he no longer works for the company, and now, months later, we have this murder spree."

He looked at Katie and could see from her expression that she was as fired up as he was.

"What's his address? Does he stay nearby?"

"I’m going to call the company and find out.”

Leblanc picked up the phone and dialed the number of the local sales office.

A young woman answered within two rings.

“Equest Pro. How can I help you?”

“It’s Detective Leblanc on the line from the cross-border task force team,” Leblanc said, making sure to emphasize his title in the hope it would speed things up. “We’re investigating a series of murders in the area and we need to question a Mr. Richard Lang, who used to work for you. I would like his home address, and also his cellphone number, if you have it.”

“Oh, that sounds terrible!” The woman seemed startled by the news. “Is that something to do with the man who was found dead yesterday? We heard about that! I can definitely help. I’m going to access his address and I’ll message it to you now. He left us a few months ago so he may have moved on, but I will give you his last recorded address when he was working as an agent, and his personal phone number."

“Thank you,” Leblanc said, reading out his number.

He killed the call, and a few moments later his phone pinged.

“Okay. We have the info. The address seems to be a smallholding, and it’s about twenty miles south of here. So it’s on the Canadian side of the border, and definitely within reach of both the ranches.”

Katie glanced back at the papers.

"There may be others, but since we can only do one at a time, and this man is the most recent that I can see, we should probably start with him."

"Let's take a drive out to his house and see if he's there," Leblanc said, feeling his blood pounding through his veins. He hoped that Richard Lang would still be living at his last recorded address. If not, at least they also had a phone number.

"His address is number three Range Road. That seems to be a long road, and very remote," Katie said, checking the map.

Again, that pointed back to the profile of person that Leblanc sensed they were seeking. Someone familiar with the wilderness, who lived in an out-of-the-way place, rather than in town.

"Let's get going. It might take us a while to find Richard, especially if he already knows we might be looking for him, Leblanc said darkly, pushing his chair back and heading for the door.

CHAPTER THIRTEEN

Half an hour after leaving Maple Ranch, Katie arrived at number three Range Road. She was driving and Leblanc was navigating, and looking out for the place they wanted. The road had started off tarred, but petered out into a rutted dirt road for the last few miles. Their SUV rocked and jolted over the uneven ground. Snow spattered the windscreen from overhanging trees as the car passed through woods that had not been cut back.

Gripping the wheel, Katie steered carefully along the rough track, hoping they would be able to find number three without a struggle, because buildings were sparse out here and signage was sporadic.

It was a wild, desolate, snowbound area and she wondered if this reflected the thoughts and character of the man who lived here.

“This must be it, up ahead. The previous one did have a number on the gate,” Leblanc said, and Katie stared expectantly at the dwelling that came into sight beyond the trees.

From the outside, the smallholding seemed tumbledown and neglected. The house looked like it had been there for a hundred years.

The front of it needed repainting, and the exterior wood was rotten and peeling. There was a huge pile of chopped wood, and partially chopped trees, in the front yard.

“There's the guy's car," Leblanc said, pointing.

It was a battered pickup which looked as though it hadn't been cleaned in years. Snow was piled on its roof.

Katie felt hopeful to see it there, as it surely meant Richard was at home.

Beyond the house, she saw a ramshackle barn a couple of hundred yards away. A few horses and cows were standing in the pasture nearby, pulling hay from a hay rack.

"Let's see if he's inside," she said, feeling a thrill of excitement that they might be coming face to face with the killer.

They climbed out of the car. Katie breathed in the smell of hay and animal manure. It was a fresh, rich scent. She headed along the path, which was inches deep in snow, and up to the front door.

Leblanc knocked on the door and they waited.

Nothing.

He knocked again, harder this time.

Katie listened, but there was no sound from inside. Was Richard there, watching them? She had an uneasy feeling that they might be watched.

"I'll try the barn," Leblanc said. “He might be down there. He must be somewhere on the property, right?” He strode purposefully down the hill toward the weathered barn.

Katie waited, feeling a growing sense of urgency, deciding to stay where she was in case he was home and decided to make a run for it.

She knocked again at the door.

"Hey, Richard. Are you home?" she shouted.

There was no answer from inside the house.

Katie hurried around to the back, wanting to check it. The back was just as unkempt as the front. There was a bedraggled vegetable patch there, with weeds in a ragged line. The back door looked as if it had been painted at the end of the previous century.

The door was locked.

She tried to peer inside, and through the dirty kitchen window, she saw a cup of coffee still steaming, and a half-finished plate of food. A half eaten egg, bacon, toast. Her eyes widened at this discovery.

He'd been there. Until very recently. And now she felt certain that it had been their arrival that had caused him to abandon his brunch.

“Leblanc, he’s here! There’s unfinished food in the kitchen,” she yelled. She saw him pause on his way to the barn, look back, and nod.

She crept back to the front of the house, wondering if he was watching from one of the windows. Where could she watch both the doors from, while Leblanc checked the barn?

As she assessed the best vantage point, she heard Leblanc let out a surprised shout.

"He's in the barn," Leblanc called. “Come quick!”

Katie turned away from the house and sprinted across the snowy yard to join him.

But, as she started running, Richard burst out of the barn.

He was astride a fit-looking bay horse. He galloped straight out of the double doorway and he and the horse veered away, heading up the hill.

"We can’t let him run!” Leblanc shouted.

They needed an urgent plan.

“You take the car!” Katie yelled, tossing the keys to him. “Then you can cut him off if he reaches a road. I’ll watch where he goes, and call you!”

Katie began running on foot, plowing through the light snow as she groped for her phone. One of them needed to keep him in sight.

Richard raced across the pasture. He turned the horse to the right and charged toward a tall barbed wire fence. There was a gate in the fence, but it was closed.

Would he slam into it, or jump it? Katie watched, feeling tense. Richard was desperate, but she didn’t want any harm to come to the horse as a result of this reckless flight.

He chose the jump. He seemed to be a skilled horseman. At just the right moment, he leaned forward, and the horse launched itself into the air at speed.

They cleared the gate easily.

Katie saw them disappear over the hill. Then she took off, her boots sinking into the snow as she ran.

She could feel the cold, damp air in her lungs, and her heart pounding harder and harder with every footstep. He couldn’t get away! Did he even know where he was going, or was he running blindly since they’d surprised him?

There was a track here! Reaching it, Katie saw it was ancient and rutted, but it was drivable and the fleeing horseman seemed to be following the route.

“Come here!” she yelled, waving to Leblanc as she rushed to the gate and dragged it open.

Behind her, she heard the car roar. Leblanc skidded through the turn, heading for the gate.

He braked hard when he reached it and she jumped inside. Leblanc accelerated along the bumpy track.

Richard galloped on without pause, heading in the direction of the large pasture on the horizon.

Leblanc was quickly gaining on him. He was driving fast, the car skidding from side to side in the snow. There was another fence ahead, but this gate wasn't jumpable. The ground in front was too damaged. It was rough, uneven and rocky, covered in fissures.

Richard wheeled the horse away from it.

Katie saw her opportunity. She was close enough.

"Stop the car!" she yelled.

Leblanc braked hard, and Katie jumped out and aimed the gun at him. She was close enough to see the horse's nostrils flaring scarlet, and the blue of Richard's eyes as he stared at her in panic. He couldn't get past this fence. The ground was too uneven. The only place he could now run was back toward the house, and they would be able to keep pace with him if he did.

"FBI and police. We need to question you. If you keep running, I'll shoot," she threatened firmly.

She could see the sweat on the horse's flanks, though the air was freezing cold. Richard looked exhausted, and he was perspiring.

But he had capitulated. He was trapped, and there was nowhere he could run.

He dismounted and walked toward them. His face was hard and suspicious. He was younger looking than Katie had expected, and he was dressed in ragged jeans and a cheap checked flannel shirt.

"Richard Lang?" she confirmed his identity.

"Yes. What do you want?" he snapped.

"Just cooperate, and we'll get this done quickly," she replied. "We have some questions to ask you about recent murders in the area."

His face closed. "I don't have time for this," he said. "I heard this morning that there was some trouble at one of the ranches, and I assumed someone else had gotten angry about the way they were treated there. I wasn't anywhere near those ranches at the time. I've been working on my own place."

He really did seem to be a man with a deep grudge against the world.

"Why did you run from us?" Katie asked.

"I figured you were probably the type to shoot first and ask questions later," he replied.

"We're here in a professional capacity, investigating a crime. But for the future, if you answer questions politely, you'll have a lot less chance of being shot than if you try to run from law enforcement," Leblanc said.

"Yeah, right," he scoffed.

"Tell us about your movements yesterday morning," Katie insisted.

The man turned to his horse and loosened the saddle cinch, rubbing his hand gently over the sweating fur.

"You suspect me?" He sighed. "I know there was trouble on the ranches. I'm - I'm not a people person. I took the job at Equest Pro because I needed cash for some repairs. I know I was rude to the ranch owners. In fact, one of them threatened to sue me because I didn't act the right way to their guests. I wasn't there to speak to guests, I was there to sell horse feed. But anyway, when I saw you here, I thought he'd sent the police and that he was going to charge me, and sue me, and I'd lose the money I made."

"Where were you yesterday morning?" Katie pressured him, wanting her question answered.

"I was fixing fences the whole morning with my neighbor. He lives a mile down the road. His name's Chuck, and you can check that with him any time. Call him now. He was there with me. We took a ride to the hardware store in town at about nine to buy a drill bit, and we also picked up some fast food and beers. I can show you everything. I have the cash slips in my jacket pocket still, inside the barn, and I spoke to a few locals in town." he insisted.

Katie glanced at Leblanc.

This suspect seemed to have an alibi even though she still wanted to confirm it properly. So, even though he was the type of person she'd imagined would fit the profile, he almost certainly hadn't committed the crime.

"Yes. Let's take a walk down there now," Leblanc said sternly. "Show me the cash slips and give me Chuck's number. I'll walk with you, so you don't get any ideas about riding away again."

Katie began heading back to the car. Disappointment filled her that this had been a dead end.

And at that moment, her phone rang. It was Scott on the line.

"I've just been notified by the Canadian police," he said. "There's a new crime scene. A guest has been murdered at Caribou Wilderness Resort, near the border. The crime's just been called in and it sounds identical. You need to get there, fast."

Katie drew in a shocked breath. "We're on our way," she said, but Scott had more to tell her. In an urgent voice, he continued.

"This is escalating, and I'm getting serious pressure from state and provincial governments on both sides of the border. They want this solved, before it affects any more of their area's prestige businesses."

This was without a doubt the highest profile case they'd yet had to solve, and Katie felt the pressure bear down on her as she rushed to the car.

CHAPTER FOURTEEN

As she and Leblanc arrived at the imposing gateway to Caribou Wilderness Resort, Katie felt stressed. This killer had struck again, and at a completely new resort. That didn't make sense, and it threw their whole logic out of line. Why was he chopping and changing locations like this, she wondered. She had no idea how he was choosing his victims.

All she knew was that, by doing so, they were ending up lagging behind him every time.

She needed to catch up with his logic, or she feared this would not be the last crime scene that they had to race to.

They reached the main lodge building. Elegant and angular, the wooden construction nestled into the side of the hill. As soon as she pulled up outside, she grabbed her winter jacket and got out. She could see two police cars parked outside the building, and a few concerned guests standing nearby, whispering to each other.

A young man in a dark blue suit arrived at the door at the same time she did. He was looking pale and shaken.

"Winter and Leblanc from the cross-border task force," she introduced them.

"I'm the manager here," he said as they shook hands briefly. "Police are at the scene. The body's still on site. Can I take you there?"

"Sure," Katie said, hoping that seeing the body on site would give her further clues.

They climbed into a smart, blue SUV, and as the manager pulled away, Katie got some basic details from him.

"The victim is a guest of about thirty. His name's Justin Gray. He was hiking with a group this morning, but according to the others, they were struggling and turned back. He went on."

"He went on alone?" Katie checked. This was an important link to the other cases.

"Yes," the manager replied. "He's a fit guy, and the others were tired, and lagging behind. They said they were glad to leave him to it. The trails are very steep up toward the mountains, and we don't get many big groups going the whole way there."

"Did he tell anyone where he was heading?" Katie asked him.

"Yes. There's only one route to the top and the whole group knew where he was headed. When he hadn't gotten back by lunch time, his girlfriend contacted me and asked if someone could go out and look for him. There's no phone reception up in the mountains so she thought he must still be there, as she couldn't get hold of him."

"Go on?" Katie said.

"We sent two of the guides to look for him. They found him immediately by the side of the track."

"How many people are staying here?" Leblanc asked.

"We have nearly fifty guests here at this time. But we've already got about half of them busy checking out and panicking about what has happened."

It occurred to Katie that there were more people here than at the other resorts, but there were also more opportunities for the killer to blend in.

The manager slowed the SUV, which had been inching up an increasingly steep slope. He parked behind a large white van that Katie guessed belonged to the police or coroner.

"From here, it's a short walk," he said.

Katie could see that the trail was a steep and rocky one. As she climbed, she felt her legs burn. Undoubtedly, the killer was fit to have climbed the whole way up here to stake out his location, she thought. She was starting to lean toward it being a man, given the level of strength that would have been necessary in every way to carry out these kills.

As she climbed, she could see swirling snow being blown by the wind. The trail wound through stretches of pine forest which was dense and dark, and the higher they walked, the thicker the snow on the ground seemed to be.

The forest was another common factor, she realized. Every kill had taken place in or near a forested area. That would provide a hiding place as well as shelter. It would also allow the killer to obscure his tracks more easily, she guessed.

The manager led them to a group of people huddled around the side of the trail. Katie heard the crackle of police walkie-talkies ahead.

"The special task force is here," the manager introduced them. The nearest policeman walked over, looking grim.

"I'm Officer McDougall. We've secured the scene," he said.

He signaled them to follow him and they picked their way past the group of guides, guests and police officers, who were all standing around the edge of the trail.

At the side of the track, an officer in a white forensic suit was taking photographs of a body.

Katie walked carefully toward the site. She could see the lying on the ground. Blood was spattered over the rocks and snow nearby.

The ground around the man was stained red, and he was lying perfectly still. His eyes were open, staring straight ahead. To Katie's surprise, he wasn't wearing a hat. He looked to be lean and fit.

She narrowed her eyes as she saw the same wounds on him. The deep neck wound must have killed him almost instantly, judging by the congealed blood. She guessed the other wounds had been made afterward, to look like a mauling.

Staring at him intensely, she had that same strange feeling she'd had at the other crime scenes where she'd attended a serial murder. That it was the killer she was looking at, not the victim.

This was his work, displayed in stark, bold, mocking clarity for the world to see.

His message. The only clues into his mind she had so far.

There were no signs of a struggle. This fit, agile man had died instantly by the killer's hand, she thought, with a chill. She wondered how that had happened. The killer must have surprised him, pouncing at the last possible moment. Perhaps the victim had been tired by that stage, resting before the final push to the top.

"How long has he been dead?" Katie asked Officer McDougall.

"The guide found him an hour ago. Coroner estimates he's been dead about four hours."

"Did he see anyone else around here?" Leblanc asked.

"No. But unfortunately, not many people take this trail line."

"Any footprints?"

"Not clear ones, no. But if you look here, you can see that there are obscured prints leading down from the top. The victim's prints are clear up until the scene."

Carefully, he led them around to take a look.

The faint indentations in the snow must have been swept over to hide them, she thought.

"The killer must have come down from the top of the trail," Katie said.

"The top of the trail makes sense," the officer agreed. "We've already been up and combed the area, but couldn't find anything, or any clear prints."

Katie nodded. This showed familiarity with the area as well as patience, she thought. Going up ahead of the group must mean he knew the ranch, and its terrain, well.

Not wanting to get in the way of the team, she moved further down the trail, looking with a sense of sadness at the deep, regular prints that Justin had made.

From the spacing, she guessed he'd been running. But here, they looked closer together. He'd slowed. Perhaps to admire the scenery. Or perhaps because he'd seen the killer ahead.

"Why here?" Leblanc said.

Katie frowned.

She walked around the scene, trying to connect the dots in her head. She knew what Leblanc meant. He wasn't talking about the location itself, which was similar to the others. He was asking: why this ranch?

It was an apt question to ask. The patterns were similar but the locations were all dissimilar. Why this victim? Why was he chosen?

She knew the answer to that was going to be the key to catching this killer, so she needed to unlock this riddle.

"It's an expensive region," Leblanc said. "Expensive travel. Expensive food. Expensive activity. Perhaps he's targeting ranches that have money? He wants to destroy the businesses somehow?"

Looking at the scene, she tried to tune into his thinking.

"I think you're right. He seems to be starting off by choosing locations," she decided. "He's picking a ranch, staking it out, and waiting for the right set of circumstances, which is a guest on their own. We need to ask the police to warn all the ranches in this area that he's working according to this pattern. Every ranch needs to take safety precautions immediately."

She saw Leblanc's eyes light up and knew that her words must have given him an idea.

"I agree. He's only striking once at each location - so far anyway, and then moving on. Perhaps if we look at the ranches that have been hit so far, now that we have three, we can see if there's a geographical pattern to the sequence that he's choosing."

Katie felt resolve build inside her.

"If we can do that, we might just predict where he'll strike next," she agreed.

CHAPTER FIFTEEN

"Can we set up shop and do some work somewhere in your main building?" Leblanc asked the manager. He was waiting for them further down the snowy slopes, shifting from foot to foot, looking cold and deeply worried.

"Of course," he said, seemingly glad to get away from the unpleasant crime scene.

They slipped and slid down the steep slope back to the SUV and climbed inside. Leblanc's mind was racing with the possibilities.

"Do you have a map of the area, or a list of the other ranches in the vicinity?" Katie asked as he eased the car down the steep road.

"Yes, I have a map," the manager said. "We actually have a purpose-designed map of the wider area, with all the ranches pinpointed. There's a company that creates it every year for tourism purposes. They also have a website. All the guest ranches pay to be featured on it."

"That sounds great," Leblanc said.

"Excuse me for asking, but will there be any more murders?" the manager said anxiously. "My guests are getting scared."

"So far, he has not struck more than once at each ranch," Leblanc said, sadly acknowledging that once was enough to destroy a business, for the season at least. "The police are calling around to all the ranches in the area to warn them. In particular, you need to ask your guests not to go out on the trails unaccompanied as so far, it's people on their own that have been targeted."

"I'll do that," the manager said seriously.

He pulled up outside the ranch building, and they hurried in through the dark, wooden doors.

The interior was a modern combination of open spaces and cozy nooks, well furnished with gleaming leather chairs and couches and polished tables. In a huge fireplace on the far wall, a log fire blazed.

Despite the warmth of the room and the sumptuous décor, there was an uneasy atmosphere in the place. At the reception desk, four guests were making a big fuss, complaining about the risk to their safety as they checked out.

The manager grimaced as he glanced their way.

"They're the fifth group of guests today to be leaving," he muttered. "People don't expect this, on a luxury vacation. This will destroy us."

Leblanc nodded grimly. The pressure was on. Jobs, and businesses, as well as lives, were at stake.

The manager led them into a private dining room with a table, a coffee machine, wi-fi, and comfortable seating. The room was warm and Leblanc felt his face glowing after the cold of the outdoors.

"I'll get that map," he said, and hurried out to fetch it.

Katie and Leblanc sat down and waited for him. The room was well decorated and inviting, with a thick rug and a polished sideboard, and paintings of mountains on the walls.

"This place is beautiful," Katie said, looking around. Leblanc knew she was thinking along the same lines as him. There was a lot at stake here.

The door opened and the manager came down the hallway with a rolled-up sheet of paper.

"Here we go," he said, and spread it out over the coffee table.

The map was pretty and colorful. It pinpointed each of the luxury ranches. Looking at it, Leblanc's first impression was that there were a lot of them. He could see why pressure was being brought to bear on their task force. These were big, profitable and influential businesses.

"Not all of them are primarily for tourism," the manager explained. "We have some large-scale cattle ranches and farms that are also on the map as they are part of the area's business network. You'll see that the tourism ones are marked with a small gold star."

Leblanc saw. However, he also noted that there weren't many without a star. It didn't reduce the numbers by much.

A thought occurred to him as he stared down, ready to map out the crime scenes so far.

"Are all these businesses still viable? Did any of them fail recently?"

He saw the quick turn of Katie's head. She clearly thought this was an excellent question. Perhaps an angry businessman, having lost money, was seeking to destroy what he thought of as his competition.

This was a possibility, and one that they needed to explore.

"That's a bit of a dark subject," the manager said. "But it's true that a few of them had a bad season and went under. In a couple of cases, their owners were forced to sell out to a competitor."

Katie and Leblanc shared a significant look.

"There was one recently that went under, leaving the owner bankrupt and even facing court charges."

"What was the name?" Katie asked. "Is this the most recent one to have closed?"

"Evergreen Ranch," the manager replied. "It's the most recent one that I know of, and it shut down in the fall."

Leblanc saw it was still listed on the map. Evergreen Ranch was on the US side, in northern Montana, and looked to be about seventy miles from where they were.

Studying the map, Leblanc realized that this failed ranch was definitely within the wider circle of those that had been targeted so far.

"Is the owner still on site?"

"I think he might be, as the business hasn't been officially sold yet."

"Okay. Any others in this area?"

"Not recently. Two others closed their doors at the end of winter last year, but they were probably a couple of hundred miles away. And a ranch in Canada acquired a neighboring one, but the owners were retiring," the manager explained. "There's also been a couple of amalgamations, with ranches acquiring more land from people who are selling up. That's all I know about, but we do hear things quite fast via the grapevine, usually."

"Thanks," Leblanc said.

The man's phone rang and with an apologetic nod, he hurried out.

"I think one of us needs to follow up on the failed business and track the owner," Leblanc said.

Katie nodded.

"I'll do that. It will save time if you continue with the mapping, while I go and speak to the owner of Evergreen Ranch."

"Okay," Leblanc said. "But if you need my help, I'll join you."

Katie was already on her feet, ready to go.

"If necessary, I'll get in touch," she said, and hurried out.

Returning to the map, Leblanc plotted out the three crime scenes and their locations. The first one was in southern Canada. The second in northern Montana. The third one was another Canadian business. If the killer was using the same map, where would he strike next, Leblanc pondered.

Of course, he might strike randomly and for no real reason.

Or he might strike wherever he could find the best tourist ranches to hit.

But Leblanc didn't think that was likely. The killer might not be operating at random. There must be a pattern, or at any rate, an area in which he felt familiar and could move with ease.

His finger traced the roadways that ran through the area. They were easy to follow on the map.

Leblanc's finger moved over the roads. And then he stopped.

There was something familiar about the roads. He couldn't quite place it. He stared at the map for a bit, allowing the image to sink into his mind, then he suddenly got it.

So far, the affected ranches formed three points within a rough square. So if the killer was going by the map, what would the fourth corner of the square be?

He drew in the fourth point. It was between the first murder site in Canada and the second one in Montana, on the Montana side of the border.

He stared at the map and felt that he had just solved another puzzle. If there was a geographical pattern to the killing, he had found it.

The name of the ranch was Windrush Stud.

He needed to contact the ranch, and to get on site there, as fast as he could.

If Leblanc was in time, they might be able to prevent another death, or even set a trap for the killer.

CHAPTER SIXTEEN

Forty-five minutes later, Leblanc pulled up outside a large wooden gateway with a big, new-looking signboard. This was Windrush Stud. He'd called the stud before he'd started driving, to explain that they might be at risk. Leblanc was glad to see that they had already acted fast.

Two SUVs were stopped at the gate and four men were waiting there. They were armed with handguns, Leblanc saw as he climbed out.

The tallest man stepped forward. He looked about fifty years old, warmly wrapped in a parka and wearing heavy boots.

"You're the detective who called us earlier? I'm the owner, Martin Franks. This is my ranch manager. And these are two of my cowboys that we've put onto security duty for the moment. So, what's the story here? These killings sound very serious. Why are we being targeted?"

"We don't know for sure that this person is coming specifically to Windrush Stud," Leblanc explained. "But based on the last three murders, it might be a good idea for us to take all precautions, in case he is working according to a geographic plan."

"Okay," Franks said. "What do you advise? Shall we get into one of the cars, so we can speak out of the wind?"

"Good idea," Leblanc said.

He climbed into one of the SUVs and Franks scrambled into the passenger seat.

"It's a long way to the ranch itself. It's a mile further up the hill. So it might be quicker to talk here," he explained.

"You need to keep a lookout for any strangers on your ranch," Leblanc advised him.

Franks nodded. "We know who's around most of the time. Anybody who's a stranger would be noticed."

"Only if he was in areas where your staff go," Leblanc cautioned.

Staring into the ranch, he saw on the horizon that a group of six horses and riders were heading out into the snow. He was glad that the ranch was taking the safety precautions and keeping people in larger groups, as he had advised.

"Should we organize a search of the ranch?" Franks asked.

"That would be a good idea. You need to pay particular attention to your walking paths, your ski trails, your horse riding trails. This killer seems to wait in forested areas and single out guests on their own, so check all trails that bypass a forest."

"I'll do that," Franks said decisively. "We do have many miles of trails, though. We won't be able to search the whole area within a day."

But Leblanc had more questions that he hoped might lead them to the killer.

"Do you know of any trouble makers in the area?" he asked. "Anyone recently fired, anyone who's caused any problems here in the past?"

Franks sighed.

"We do have a problem neighbor. I'm not sure if that's helpful? His name's Rodney Hodge."

"Tell me about him?" Leblanc asked.

"I don't want to cause any worse issues," Franks said hesitantly. "I don't want to get into a feud."

"It's okay. We're looking to make sure he's not a suspect. We want to eliminate him from the investigation. So it's better to know about him. If he's innocent, you'll be helping us get to the real cause of these murders."

"He runs a small ranch that borders ours to the north. He's a bit of a recluse, and he's been very verbally abusive in the past to guests who've accidentally crossed the border into his farm. He used to own another place in northern Montana, which he sold a few months ago, and he behaved the same way when he was there, apparently."

"I see," Leblanc said. "So he's known for being hostile."

"Yes. So we all steer clear of him. His farm doesn't cater for guests, and if they do end up there by mistake, we tell them to get back over to our place and try not to engage with him. Even then, we've had problems with him. He seems to have a grudge against the ranch and the company. He's an unpleasant person to deal with. I've been very close to calling the police out in the past. Only problem being the police are not close by and it seemed excessive to do so."

"I'll take a drive there," Leblanc said.

"It's about five miles up the road. You'll see the signboard at the gate," the owner advised.

Leblanc got back into his own car and headed north on the road, keeping a lookout for the entrance to Rodney Hodge's property. He felt eager that this might finally be getting somewhere. A property owner with a grudge could be significant, and more importantly, this man's protected territory lay squarely within the killing zone so far. As an owner of multiple farms, he could have issues with many of the locals.

The road veered to the right, and he drove for another two miles along a very rutted dirt track. Then ahead he saw a wooden gate and the sign he'd been expecting.

"R. Hodge Cattle & Ranching. No Trespassers. By Appointment Only."

The gate was closed. Clearly, Rodney didn't want visitors. But there was no phone number, so Leblanc pushed it open and drove in, getting out to close it behind him.

A few hundred yards ahead, he saw the ranch buildings. They were more modest than Windrush, but the ranch seemed busy. Cattle and horses were out in the pastures.

He drove up to the main building, a large, wooden house.

Wind swirled around him. Apart from the lowing of the cattle, the place was very quiet.

Where was Rodney, Leblanc wondered, feeling spooked and a little nervous to be treading on the property of an unfriendly and unpredictable neighbor.

He banged on the front door. There was no response. Leblanc could hear dogs barking from inside.

Leblanc walked around the side of the house, thinking that he would see Rodney somewhere in one of the yards. But there was no one to be seen.

He knocked again, at the back door.

Still no reply.

But then, from behind him, his blood chilled as he heard a sound he knew only too well.

It was the harsh, metallic sound of a pump-action shotgun being readied.

"What the hell are you doin'?" a furious voice shouted.

Leblanc's heart raced.

Slowly, he turned, not wanting to spook the man and get shot.

As he raised his hands, trying to bring some calm to a situation that could turn deadly at any moment, he saw Rodney Hodge standing a dozen feet away.

He was a big man, in his late fifties, with a puffy face and an angry expression. He was aiming a shotgun directly at Leblanc's chest.

"You got no business bein' here," Hodge shouted. "Did you not read the sign at the gate? No trespassers. Now get off my property."

"I'm a police detective. I'm going to lower my hands and open my jacket to show you my badge," Leblanc said calmly, knowing that his credentials would probably not help the situation. Sure enough, Rodney's frown deepened.

If he was face to face with the killer, Leblanc strongly suspected he wouldn't hesitate to shoot.

Feeling as if he was treading an unsteady tightrope, Leblanc lowered his hands and slowly opened his jacket.

"Put the gun down. I'm a cop. If you shoot, there are going to be serious consequences," Leblanc said, knowing that if he was facing the killer, he wouldn't care.

Fighting for calmness, Leblanc produced his badge. He wished he'd thought to tell Katie where he was going. He'd never dreamed that he would end up face to face with a cowboy who was gun-happy, violent and unstable, who clearly had huge issues with the neighboring farms, and who could well be the killer they were hunting.

It felt like eons before Rodney lowered the gun.

"I've had enough of the cops," he snapped. "The last time they came out here was to arrest me on a trumped up charge of assault. A cowboy got drunk and fell over. I asked him to leave my property, and he turned violent. So I defended myself. And the next thing I know, the cops were swarming all over my property," he grumbled.

Leblanc was simply relieved he no longer had to look into the dark eye of that powerful shotgun.

"I need to ask you a few questions. There have been murders in the area," he explained.

"I have nothing to do with any murder. Are you mad, accusing me like that?"

"We heard you have had problems with guests in nearby ranches. That you've threatened them," Leblanc insisted.

"I just don't want people coming onto private property and interfering here. These guests who come to these ranches think they own everything. I've had gates opened, cattle out in the road, even a mare injured as a result of their thoughtless interference."

"I need to account for your movements over the past couple of days," he said firmly.

Rodney glared at him. His eyes were bloodshot, and his face was a network of broken veins.

"You're trying to trick me. Force me into a confession of some kind. I know the way your type works. I'm a good, honest rancher. I just want to live my life, like everyone else."

"I'm not out to trick you. I simply want to confirm an alibi," Leblanc said, feeling that the more calmness he could bring to this situation, the easier it would be to get what he needed.

"I was here the past few days. I went out to town yesterday afternoon. That's it."

"Were you here on your own?"

"My men were here, too," he said finally. Leblanc had the sense he was coming down from his pedestal of defiance, and beginning to act in a more reasonable way. "You can ask them. We had the vet out yesterday morning to geld four of the horses. He was here all morning with me. We use McCarthy. His surgery's in town. Then this morning, we've been busy with the cattle in the crush, doing deworming and medications. We're a busy, working ranch, and that's why I don't have time for interference."

He turned, and Leblanc saw two men had emerged from behind an outbuilding and were regarding them anxiously.

"Joe. Brent. What have we been doing this morning?" Rodney asked.

"We've been working cattle," the closest man called back. "Up in the main pasture. Running them through the crush to medicate them."

"And yesterday morning?"

"We had the vet here to geld the colts," the man called back. "Why are you asking? You were there, boss!"

"Okay," Leblanc said. "That should be all I need from you."

Now that he was off the hook, Rodney seemed marginally warmer to him.

"It's these fancy ranches round about that have caused all our issues," he suggested. "Big money attracts big trouble. That's what I've always said. We're down to earth here. Normal folk. We keep to ourselves and don't want interference."

"I understand," Leblanc said, anxious to be on his way. "And please, take care. Until this killer is caught, everyone should be careful."

Leblanc turned back to his car, feeling a mixture of relief and trepidation.

Rodney had seemed like a strong suspect, but with an alibi for the past two mornings, he was off the hook.

This confrontation had reminded him that among the people living in these isolated areas, there were definitely more than the usual number of trigger-happy survivalists with little regard or respect for the law.

Katie, too, had been headed on a dangerous mission and with a jolt, he realized she hadn't yet called. Worried, Leblanc dialed her number. His concern grew as he listened to it ring and ring unanswered.

CHAPTER SEVENTEEN

The hour and a half drive to Evergreen Ranch that Katie had anticipated, took closer to two hours, because the roads in the last stretch were damaged. A crew was working, doing temporary repairs to patch the crater-like potholes, and a stop-start system was in place.

Finally, she pulled up outside the ranch.

Katie saw immediately what just a few months of neglect had done in these harsh conditions.

Whereas the rest of the ranches in the area were neat and well-kept, this one looked unkempt and uncared for. Tall weeds and grasses had grown over the verges, and the overgrowth was visibly tangled against the gatepost, in areas where the snow hadn't settled. Even the paint on the sign was faded, and the sign itself was rattling in the wind.

The wheels of her SUV crunched over the deeply eroded gravel drive as she headed inside.

The ranch house itself, which must have once been grand, was in a somewhat similar state of disrepair. As she approached, she saw the white paintwork was peeling, the shutters were loose and the windows were filthy. There was no furniture on the wide front porch, which she guessed would have made a magnificent breakfast spot for guests in summer.

There were several outbuildings nearby which looked to have been guest accommodation, but they didn't seem to be in use. Although the buildings were large and spacious, Katie saw dirty glass, one window smashed. The paths leading between them were barely visible through the snow, and looked poorly maintained. The doors were either closed, or hanging off their hinges.

The pastures were overgrown, with broken fences, and apart from a few wild birds, she didn't see a single animal in sight.

Or any humans either. Katie shivered. This place felt like a ghost town.

Katie got out of her SUV. Her boots crunched over the snow as she made her way towards the ranch house. The place was completely still.

She looked around uncertainly. She couldn't see a soul, and felt a fluttering unease. Wrapping her jacket tightly around her, she headed up to the house, ringing the bell.

The sound of the chimes echoed through the house.

When there was no response, she rang again, and then knocked hard on the door.

There was no sound or movement inside.

But when she glanced to the right, she noticed an ancient car, hidden away under the lean-to behind the nearest building. It was an old pickup that must have done many miles, but it was clear of snow and the windshield had been wiped. And now she noticed that the snow between the car and the house looked disturbed.

Someone did live here, in this desolate farm. And that person must be at home. Katie had no idea if it was the original owner or whether a tenant – official or otherwise – might have moved into this farm.

She shivered. It really did feel spooky out here, with the blustering wind and the rattling sign and the hints at the presence of people who were nowhere to be seen.

Then, from inside the house, she heard a crash.

Had it been a door slamming? Something smashing? The noise had definitely come from within this dilapidated home.

"Hello!" she yelled. "Is everything okay in there?"

Tentatively, she took hold of the handle and pushed the front door. It swung open easily, and Katie stepped inside.

"FBI!" she called. "Is there anyone in here?"

The hall had the same peeling paint on the walls as the outside. The floor was dark wood but she saw footprints, as if snowy feet had trod inside recently. On the far side of the hall, a pair of boots was lying on the floor.

Katie headed across the hall, shivering, because the house was cold and drafty. There was a big room to her right that must have been used for reception, or perhaps a lounge, but it was empty and freezing cold. The fireplace at the far side was bare. It was a long time since flames had flickered in that grate.

But then, she stopped dead, her heart accelerating as she heard a sound.

It was the faint but distinct scuffle of footsteps.

Turning away from the lounge, Katie sprinted through the house.

She found herself in the kitchen. The room was huge, with a wood stove at the far end, but the counters were bare. Beyond, she saw a long dining table surrounded by chairs and covered in dust.

She hurried through to the next room, a sunroom, with a large glass front that must have seen spectacular views in the summer, but which now just let in the icy chill and cutting wind.

There were more footprints here. They ran up to the back door, which was ajar, blowing in the breeze.

Katie paused, trying to listen, but she didn't hear anyone.

Moving quickly through the sunroom, Katie headed for the back door, her heart thudding in her ears. Where had the footsteps headed? It sounded, and looked, as if someone had rushed out of the house via the back door, but she had no idea what their intentions were. Had it just been to get away from her, had they gone out for some other reason?

Or were they waiting outside for her to emerge?

She didn't like the last idea at all. She drew her gun. Then, pushing the door wider, she stepped out.

The yard was small, a few feet of ice-covered grass, with an open shed at the back.

She headed toward the shed with all her instincts prickling.

At that moment, there was a rustle of movement in the trees behind her and Katie swung around, just as a dark figure burst out.

It was a tall, burly man, dressed in jeans and a jacket, and was bareheaded.

He wasn't looking at Katie. He was fleeing away from her, running as fast as he could in the direction of the old car.

"Hey!" she cried. "What are you doing? Stop right there."

The man didn't stop. He just ran faster, heading toward the car.

Katie set off, in hot pursuit, her feet pushing through the uneven snow. He glanced over his shoulder, looking shocked.

"Stop! FBI!" she screamed.

Katie was closing in. She could hear his labored breathing ahead as he raced around the far side of the ranch house. He was making for the car.

Her own car was all the way around the other side of the house. If this jalopy started up first time, he could be down the drive and on the road before she was behind the wheel. She couldn't let him drive off.

He had a lead on her, but he didn't have his keys out, and she saw him fumble for them in his pocket as he ran. That slowed him down and gave her the chance to sprint closer.

He tried to scramble up into the driver's seat, but she was gaining on him, and he wasn't fast enough.

Katie was almost upon him, but he was just ahead of her. He made it into the car. She feared he was going to slam the door and get away. Frantically, she dived for him, grabbing at his jacket, and her fingers were so numb with the cold, it was a moment before she realized – he was caught.

He was trapped. She had him.

Wild-eyed and breathing heavily, he stared at her.

"What the hell-?" he started.

"Don't move your hands!" Katie said, wondering if he had a weapon in that heavy jacket that he might go for, now that he was cornered. "I'm an officer of the law. I clearly identified myself, and you disobeyed a direct instruction to stop. Get out of the car and get down on the ground. Do it now."

Her voice was powerful as she barked out her command.

But the man didn't move. He just sat there, his eyes popping in disbelief.

"I'm not kidding. Get out and get down on the ground," she repeated.

When he still didn't move, Katie reached forward, grabbing his shoulder and pulling him towards her.

"Ow! You're hurting me. You're hurting me!" he protested. She saw the fight and the resistance ebbing from him. Probably, it had been fueled by the adrenaline of the chase.

"I will do more than hurt you if you don't listen to me," Katie insisted. "Get out of the car. Get down on the ground. Now."

She made sure to keep her gun trained on him, but also well out of reach of a sudden grab.

On the ground! On your belly, now! Hands behind your back."

Katie kept her gun at the ready as he obeyed, his gloved hands in the snow.

He was panting, his eyes wide.

The second he was out, she reached into the car and snatched the keys out of the ignition.

"What's this about?" he asked, panic in his face as she patted him down. He didn't have a weapon on him. Katie relaxed slightly but she didn't lower her gun.

"What's your name?"

"Ben Jessop."

"Are you the owner here?"

"Yes. Yes, I owned this place. It's been foreclosed, though."

"I'm here because of a string of murders that have taken place in the surrounding area in the past few days," Katie told him sternly.

To her surprise, his face relaxed.

"Oh. Oh, is that it? I - I didn't know about them. I haven't been around anyone for a few days."

"What did you think I was here for, Mr. Jessop?" Katie asked in a hard voice, wanting to get to the truth of why he'd run.

"You know, the police have been after me because - well, there was a fire in one of the outbuildings just before we closed our doors. The insurance company investigated and they deemed it as arson. So they've been threatening to sue me for insurance fraud," he explained unhappily.

Things sure hadn't been going well for Mr. Jessop, Katie thought.

In her pocket, her phone started buzzing, but she didn't take the call. She was too focused on getting an alibi from this suspect, while he was in the mindset to talk.

"Where were you this morning? And yesterday morning?" she asked. "Can you account for your movements?"

"This morning I was here, on the farm. Yesterday, I was in town. I had a meeting with my lawyer," he said. He craned his neck, staring up at her, looking uncomfortable mentally as well as physically.

"Which lawyer? What time?"

"The meeting was at eleven. With Patrick Callahan and Associates, in Butte." He glanced at his car again.

Butte was a good hundred and fifty miles away, Katie reckoned. The journey would have taken him three hours in each direction. That ruled out his presence in the area yesterday and that meant he could not have been at Diamond Ice ranch when Banks was killed.

So he had an alibi for at least one of the murders. If that checked out, Katie was satisfied that he was not their man. There was no evidence that more than one person was involved in these crimes, especially with the oddly shaped wounds which all seemed to be made by the same knife, one that might have been bent or twisted in some way.

"Give me your lawyer's details," she said.

He scrambled to his knees and delved in his jacket pocket, producing a business card.

"Do you know of any other businesses nearby that have gone under?" she asked him, deciding that as an affected person, he might have heard of others which she didn't yet know about.

He shook his head. "Nothing in this area. I was the only unfortunate one. Everyone else had a good season, I think."

"How about your workers, or your managers? Did anyone end up in difficult circumstances, which might have made them angry?"

"No. They were all experienced people. Nobody suffered. Everyone found jobs elsewhere."

"Okay," Katie said, deciding that there was no need to question him further. "Next time the police come around, don't run. I can tell you from personal experience, it doesn't help and only makes you look guilty.

Looking embarrassed, Jessop nodded.

Katie turned and went back to her car. This had been a long drive and she'd hoped for a better outcome.

As soon as she climbed in, she checked her phone, seeing that Leblanc had called. Quickly she called him back.

"Katie. You okay?" He sounded anxious.

"Yes. All good. However, this suspect had an alibi. How about you?"

"I'm at the ranch that I think might be next on the list, if the killer is working on the geographic locations and he's going according to a pattern. There's no sign of him yet but everyone's on high alert. Do you want to join me here? They're busy with a hunt for the killer and are going to search until it gets dark."

"I'll be there as soon as I can," Katie said, hoping that the hunt would uncover the killer - or at least delay his deadly agenda before he murdered again.

CHAPTER EIGHTEEN

M smiled as the scene came into focus in his powerful binoculars. Sharp. Crystal clear. Better than real life. He'd picked the perfect vantage point here. He was hidden behind scrub, up the side of the mountain, with the valley spread out before him.

He could see a woman going into her cabin. Tall, slender, confident. A ray of sunshine briefly pierced the gathering clouds, highlighting her pale, shining hair and the sparkle of jewelry at her throat.

She looked to be in her late forties, with a compact body and wide, expressive eyes and he closed in on her face. Surprisingly, there wasn't the sour, evil expression he'd expected to see. Instead, she was smiling.

Lowering the binoculars, he checked his environment. The forest was quiet now. He'd heard voices earlier but nobody had come close to his secluded spot.

He saw nothing that would stop him. Relishing the opportunity, he raised the binoculars again and took another look at the woman, watching her as she walked past the cabin's open door. If she turned on the lights, it would be like viewing somebody on stage. He was patient and could wait.

Methodical.

Mindful.

He smiled. He'd see her every move from here, whether she was in a room or at the window. And all the while she'd be unaware of his presence.

He flicked open his case, revealing the knife with its crude, warped blade. He took it out, stroking the steel with his finger, being careful because it was very sharp.

Returning his focus to the cabin, he saw the woman's eyes narrow and she turned to glance over her shoulder, as if somehow sensing something was out of place. Or perhaps someone inside was calling to her. For a strange moment he wondered if she was being warned about him.

But M knew there was nothing to be afraid of. He need not be paranoid. He was hidden away here, and was just a watcher. A spectator.

He frowned, as the memories returned. He'd been treated unfairly. He'd been labeled a stalker. They had called him a peeping Tom, these rich folk who held their privacy around them like it was some kind of personal right.

He felt the anger burn and fester. How unfairly they had treated him! He was going to make them pay again and again for what they had done.

Swinging the binoculars around, he focused on another part of the ranch, watching two guests arrive.

They were laughing and joking, happy. Well, why wouldn't they be, so shielded from reality by their immense wealth?

He watched, narrowing his eyes as they strode past one of the housemaids without even looking in her direction. They didn't see her, it was as if she didn't exist in their world.

Like the woman he had watched earlier, this couple was dressed in expensive clothes.

He focused on them, watching the man's face, seeing in his eyes the superiority he'd expected to find.

The anger burned within him. He hoped they would decide to go out on the trails. Not both of them, of course. Only one. He wouldn't even mind which one it was. Neither one looked particularly strong. He wasn't picking on strong people because he didn't want to be hurt and couldn't risk being injured. Rather, he was choosing women, or men who showed a sign of weakness. Elderly. Asthmatic. Or else doubled over with muscle cramps.

A smile spread across his face as he felt the excitement grow.

There was nothing better than watching the game and anticipating the kill.

He would make them feel fear. He would show them how fragile life was so that they truly understood the meaning of hardship. No more entitlement and arrogance.

They needed to learn respect, and to be shown that they weren't any better than him. That was what he was looking forward to teaching them.

He would show them that they were no one. It was going to happen soon. He could feel it.

His whole body was buzzing with anticipation as he moved the binoculars around, scanning the valley.

It was so easy to spot them, and from these vantage points, even easier to watch them. He was an expert at picking the perfect lookout points. How he loved to view these guests while they didn't know he was looking, to swing the binoculars round from place to place, feeling the familiar tightening of excitement as he identified the right target.

No one saw him. No one knew he was here. He was careful and cautious, he planned and he made sure.

Method. Not Madness.

He checked his surroundings once again, but the forest was quiet now. He would hear if any footsteps approached, but he knew they couldn't, because they would first have to walk along the sweeping pathway that was clearly within his view.

He saw nothing that would stop him.

He caressed his knife once more, admiring the craftsmanship. Even though it was rough and lacked finesse, it was his blade that he had made.

It felt ice cold as he pressed it lightly against his cheek. That was because his vantage point was frigid. M had learned to be strong and withstand the cold, as he stayed in one place for hours.

He was tough and strong. He could handle the wait. Of course, he was prepared to stay out here until the job was done. There was no need to rush. He had all day. He was in no rush. He could wait until dark if necessary.

"I don't mind waiting for you, honey," he murmured.

Would the blonde go out alone? He wasn't sure she was as nice as she had led him to believe. Taking another look, he was sure that she was just as arrogant and entitled as the others. She'd just been fooling him, with that happy smile. He watched her head along the walkway to the ranch's main building.

There was a man sweeping the path. M watched entranced to see what she would do.

Sure enough, she looked at him as if he was dirt. M felt anger well up inside. How dare she look like that. How dare she be so superior.

He felt his blood race.

The blonde was headed for the stables, and he watched, his anticipation building as she strode there. She barely nodded at the wrangler in the parka and cowboy hat, who was holding the horses.

They were prepared and waiting. They looked sleek and fit, their coats gleaming.

He was sure a woman like this would ride out on her own.

But to his surprise, she mounted up and rode off to join a small group of others. And then the wrangler himself swung his leg over the final horse and cantered off to join them.

A group ride wouldn't work for him. Again, too much risk that he'd be caught. That was a pity because he had looked forward to taking someone from a horse. Particularly her.

Still, there would be another opportunity, he had no doubt.

His body might be cold and stiff but that was no matter. It was a price worth paying, because it was important to wait for the right moment.

But as he stared down at the ranch, swinging his binoculars from point to point, M realized something strange.

Nobody was heading out on their own. Not as yet, anyway. Everyone who was leaving the immediate area of the ranch building and chalets was doing so in small groups of four or more people.

He felt an unexpected stab of fear.

Surely it couldn't be? Had they been warned? Had word already gotten out about what he was doing?

Panic flared briefly within him. He'd thought that thanks to his artistry and skill, they wouldn't realize it was the work of a human but rather an animal kill. He'd known that eventually this might happen, but had assumed he'd have much more time.

Frantically, he told himself there was no need to be alarmed or give up. The wealthy folk believed they were invulnerable. The more arrogant ones wouldn't listen to warnings and would do what they wanted anyway, he was relying on that.

He told himself firmly to be patient. Even if they were being careful for now, he would find another way. He would wait and watch and then strike when they least expected it.

That was what he needed. Another way. If they were changing things up, then he would too, and he had the perfect idea of what to do.

Snow was falling. He liked snow. It always brought with it invisibility and opportunity.

He backed away to the safety of the trees and then he was gone.

CHAPTER NINETEEN

Leblanc felt huge relief when he saw Katie's car pull up outside Windrush Stud. Splitting up to check out possible leads had been necessary to save time, but it was always riskier.

Again, the memory of Cecile loomed in his mind. He'd left her to go to the prison on her own, and look what had happened. Leblanc knew he couldn't let his past affect his present and he must not allow old trauma to influence his approach to his work.

But even so, he couldn't help the worry that flared automatically inside him whenever his investigation partner headed out alone. Going their separate ways, they'd both encountered risk. It had not gotten them closer to the killer, and now the sky was darkening as a storm swept in.

"They've offered to put us up here for the night," he said as she got out of the car. "It makes sense, I think. The police have warned all the ranches close to this one. Everyone is going to be on the alert and making sure guests don't go out alone."

"That's good," she replied. "It means we'll be in the area."

She didn't need to say any more. Leblanc knew what she meant. They would be in the area, and close by, if the killer struck again.

That might be a worst-case scenario but it was a grim reality since their leads so far had all petered out.

"You mentioned there was a search in progress?"

Leblanc nodded. "There was, but they called it off. It looks like the weather is closing in and there will be heavy snow just now. It's set to clear after dark."

Glancing at the sky, he saw Katie nod.

"That might be to our advantage. It will hopefully drive him indoors," she said.

Together, they walked to the ranch's main building.

"They've given us two chalets," Leblanc said. "Numbers thirty and thirty-one. Mine has a lounge area. Actually, they probably both do. Shall we sit down and review what we have found?"

"Sure," Katie said.

He handed her the keycard for thirty-one and headed down the winding path to the right of the main building. The chalets were well spaced out with guest privacy clearly a concern. Even so, Leblanc couldn't help feeling uneasy as he walked, as if there was someone watching him. When the first big flakes of snow began to fall, he was relieved.

He unlocked the door of his chalet and stepped inside.

He needed to work out what they'd missed. What they were missing.

He wanted to make the best of a bad situation, but he couldn't ignore the sense of failure that burned inside him. They'd had a whole day. It had passed and they hadn't made the progress he'd hoped for.

The chalet was comfortably warm and inviting. The lounge area included a small dining room table for two, a sofa, an armchair, and a coffee table. A log fire burned merrily in one corner.

They sat down at the dining room table. He glanced up as the wind battered the window glass.

"I think we need to scout out the higher lying areas," Katie said. "The problem is that there are so many of them. These ranches are huge and they're all forested and mountainous. But he must be waiting somewhere to identify the right victim."

Leblanc nodded. "I think he might. It makes sense for him to be at the highest point. A place that people don't frequent. The higher the better."

"And close to a forest."

"Yes. All the kill sites have been close to a forested area. It's a hiding place for him," Leblanc said.

"Would helicopter footage work?" Katie suggested. Then she shook her head. "He'd hear it."

"Drone footage?" Leblanc suggested. "It's a big area to cover but that might be an option."

"Yes," Katie agreed. "It's definitely an option when the snow stops. Especially if we can pinpoint which ranch he's likely to be staking out."

She sighed. "I'd say all of them. He has to be flexible in his approach, right? He'll see one ranch is taking precautions and that might mean he'll chop and change in order to pick the right target."

Leblanc nodded. He really wanted to tell Katie that it was going to be okay. That he would find their man and end this killing spree. But he knew better. Out there, the killer had the advantage, and could easily change his plans. After all, they'd seen that he picked a location rather than an individual person, and that his biggest need seemed to be simply to kill.

*

It was late at night before Leblanc climbed into bed. He and Katie had eaten dinner together. It had felt strange, being served delicious food in such a high quality restaurant, knowing all the time that they were on a desperate hunt for the killer. But these ranches were offering hospitality and Leblanc knew that both food and rest were important when operating in the icy cold.

He found that he couldn't sleep. As soon as his head touched the pillow, his mind began to race.

First he went back over the day. Then he began to think of the things they still needed. Sourcing a drone, if that would even be viable in such a huge area. He'd need to research the possibility. He wanted to study the terrain, the weather. Take another look at the map.

It all added up to a lot of work.

He was trying to think, trying to piece together the next few days, but his thoughts kept returning to Cecile. He had failed her, and that was a hard fact to accept.

But when he closed his eyes, he didn't see Cecile's face in his mind. Instead, he saw Katie's. Her intense green eyes, her shiny brown hair, that mischievous grin that occasionally warmed her otherwise serious face, with its slim oval shape and the light dusting of freckles across the bridge of her nose.

With sleep eluding him, Leblanc got to his feet and pulled on his dressing gown. He was surprised to see the snow had just stopped. He'd been so involved in reviewing the case that he hadn't even noticed.

He needed a hot drink. Or maybe some fresh air would help clear his mind.

He went out onto the deck outside his chalet. The door was ajar, but he felt safe. A couple of lights shone from the main building. He saw nobody out and about. That was good.

Glancing across at Katie's chalet, he noticed her light was on. Perhaps she couldn't sleep either.

Maybe they could have a hot drink together. Leblanc felt suddenly drawn toward her, needing her companionship.

He pulled on jeans and a coat, got his feet into his boots, and walked down the short wooden staircase that led to the walkway. His breath misted in the air.

He climbed the stairs to Katie's chalet and knocked on the door.

But there was no reply.

Leblanc frowned. Her light was on. Why wasn't she answering?

Was everything okay in there?

Suddenly, there seemed to be an element of threat in the silent, snowy night.

"Katie?" he called, anxiety flaring. "Are you all right?"

He tried the door and to his shock, he found it open.

"Katie?" he called out again, louder this time.

He opened the door wider, speaking her name again loudly before peering inside.

He stepped inside, his heart racing now, his mind abuzz with all the different scenarios that might explain why she wasn't responding.

He called her name again and looked around the lounge area, noticing her cell phone on the table. Surely if she was in bed, she'd have taken it with her?

Stepping cautiously to the open bedroom door, Leblanc caught his breath as he saw her bed was empty, the covers disturbed and pushed back.

Katie was nowhere to be seen.

CHAPTER TWENTY

Katie walked through the silent, snowy landscape, her breath misting in the air as she followed the winding path.

Unable to sleep, she had decided to head to the main ranch and sit by the fire with a book. Hopefully, reading would calm down her thoughts, because at the moment they were racing. The hunt for the serial killer was causing the memories of her sister to resurface in vivid intensity.

She remembered every word of the short exchange she'd had with Everton, just a couple of weeks ago, in the maximum security prison, and what he'd said.

How she'd felt. As if he'd punched her in the gut. She had no idea what his words meant. Had he been telling the truth, dropping her a crumb? Or had he just been taunting her?

But one thing was for sure. She would never forget that day, or his words.

The more she thought about Everton, the more she felt herself reliving the past, going over it all again. It was something she was determined to avoid doing, especially during a case, but once the door was open, the memories and feelings flooded through.

She had failed to protect her sister. Her reckless, irresponsible actions had destroyed all their lives. No wonder she was still wrestling with the demons of guilt. But now, her scenario of what had happened was confused by the chance that Everton might have been telling the truth.

Katie stopped, shivering in the intense cold. Surely she should have seen the main building by now?

As she reoriented herself, she realized she'd taken the wrong turning when the pathway had branched. Now, she wasn't going toward the main building, which had not been directly visible from her chalet.

In the darkness, with low lights along the path at intervals but nothing more, she had gotten herself turned around and was heading out to the trails.

A signboard loomed ahead and for a moment, Katie was so tempted to go for a walk.

The wind blew, carrying a flurry of snowflakes.

Her boots crunched on the snow, but it crumbled easily, with little of the resistance she had assumed would be there on a night when the temperature had plummeted. She kept walking a few more steps, enjoying the sensation of being all alone, of nobody around.

But she couldn't go further. Not only would it be unsafe, but she hadn't even brought her gloves out with her and her hands were already freezing.

Reaching out, Katie touched the cold wooden pole of the sign, feeling the texture of the wood under her hand. Then she turned back, walking through the darkness, retracing her steps.

It was at that moment she heard the noise. A soft footfall.

She stopped, her heart speeding up. She'd thought she was alone out here. Yet, in this darkness, she could not be sure. Turning, she looked to see if anyone was behind her.

Nobody was there. For a moment she'd wondered if it was Leblanc, also sleepless, out for a walk the same as her. But the path was silent.

Even so, she couldn't shake off the feeling that someone was watching her, following her.

It was probably a deer, she decided. An animal must have sensed her and was now moving away from her.

But what if it wasn't?

Katie suddenly realized how reckless her behavior had been. There was a killer in the wider area. He had never struck at night. She hadn't thought he would. But the problem was that he'd been unable to single out a victim on his or her own during the day.

Katie turned around slowly, adrenaline flooding her. What was that? She saw a shadow in the trees nearby.

Was it the shadow of a man?

She moved her gaze from side to side. Was there someone there? Hidden by the trees?

At that moment, the shadow moved. It lunged toward her at speed. She saw the glint of a strange, twisted blade plunging down to her throat. She ducked away, kicking out at him in horror, but with an angry grunt he grabbed her jacket, and then Katie was fighting for her life.

She didn't have time to scream. She knew she was dead if she didn't act quickly. She saw the gleam in his eyes, filled with rage and the intensity of what he was doing. His breath huffed out, hot mist in the dark, cold air as he raised his hand again, yanking her toward him with the other.

He was impossibly strong and almost dragged her off her feet. Stumbling to keep her balance, she grabbed at the wrist of the hand holding the knife.

With that, he lunged at her again. But this time, she kicked out, hitting the killer's thigh. He stumbled, losing his balance for a moment.

She dropped and rolled as another vicious blow from the blade slashed through the air where her head had been only a moment before. This was how he struck, she realized. Fast, brutal, using speed as his weapon and attacking a target that he thought was weaker, or unaware.

Out here, with no gun and wrapped in her thoughts, had been both, and now might pay for it with her life.

As she rolled, she turned, kicking out with both feet. The man grunted, then launched a new attack. She felt the blade slice through her coat. The material ripped and tore.

She rolled again, then crouched and lunged at him. She found his knee with her hand and punched as hard as she could, hoping to hurt him or at least knock him off his feet. He used his free hand to grab at Katie's hair, pulling hard. Katie grabbed at the wrist again and this time, she held on tightly. But he was too strong for her. She knew she couldn't hold him off for long. With only seconds to spare, she needed to use the weapon that might save her, the one she could use but he could not.

Her voice.

"Help!" she yelled as loud as she could. "I'm being attacked! Help me! Come and get this guy!"

Her cries didn't deter him. His violence redoubled.

He wrapped his free arm around her neck. She felt his forearm against her throat, his grip tight and hard. Blood was rushing to her head. She tore at his arm, trying to get his stranglehold to loosen, because she knew all he was doing was trying to position her and weaken her so that the knife could tear into her throat.

At that moment, running footsteps thudded toward them.

She heard Leblanc's voice, loud and urgent.

"Katie! Where are you?"

"Here!" she tried to scream through her stranglehold.

But then, the man let go.

Katie made a desperate grab for him but her fingers were too weak. And then he was gone, plunging away into the same undergrowth he'd emerged from.

She stumbled to her feet as Leblanc arrived, his coat flapping. Gloveless and hatless, he looked stressed and anxious.

"What happened?" he asked. "Were you attacked? Are you okay?"

"I'm fine." She gasped out the words, propping herself up on wobbly legs. She was determined not to pass out before she'd gotten the important message across, even though she felt dizzy from lack of air.

"He was here. We need to chase him. Now."

That twisted blade seemed etched on her vision. She stumbled back and Leblanc hurriedly grabbed her arm, supporting her.

"You think it was the guy we need?" Leblanc sounded incredulous. "Here? At night?"

"He's changed his methods. He's never killed at night before. But he's been forced to because the ranch was being careful."

Katie gestured to the footprints, deep in the snow, that showed which way the killer had headed.

"We need to go after him. Right now!" Leblanc said, staring purposefully at the tracks.

"No, no. I'm not dressed for the cold, and can still barely breathe. I'm not going to be able to run for a while. You can't go on your own," Katie pleaded. "It's too dangerous. He knows the area, and he might be waiting for you. We can't afford to lose you, Leblanc, or for you to be hurt."

She could see Leblanc wanted to argue back, but as the truth of her words sunk in, and he heard her still-hoarse voice, he looked appalled, then guilty, and finally, angry. He gave a terse nod.

"You're not okay. I can see you're not. He almost killed you. We need to get you checked out by a medic. But you shouldn't have been out alone in the first place. Risking yourself when we're in a dangerous investigation! We can't afford to lose you!"

As he reached this conclusion, she realized he sounded angrier than she'd heard him for weeks.

"Let's sound the alarm. Organize a manhunt," she said, needing to deflect him and get things back on track. "If we move fast enough, perhaps we can find him."

CHAPTER TWENTY ONE

An hour later, the ranch was abuzz. Katie stood under the glare of the spotlights, at the point where the attack had taken place, shivering in the midnight chill. She was still aching all over and her voice was rough, but her throat was starting to feel better now that the ranch medic had treated her, and given her some medication.

From overhead, another powerful beam sent shadows sweeping around the ranch as the police helicopter arrived. The sound split the air as it hovered low, communicating with the officers on the ground standing next to Katie. Snow, swept from the leaves, whirled around in the force of the blades.

Then the helicopter veered away in the direction the killer had fled.

"He's run already," she said to Leblanc. "I know he has. He changed things up and now he's gained a huge advantage, by attacking at night."

At least she had more of a physical description, although still sketchy. He was about five-ten in height, broad shouldered, and now thanks to the footprints, they had an exact shoe size, as well as clear images of the sole tread. He'd been wearing pale, lightly patterned clothing. Snow camouflage. It would make him harder to track, she worried.

Leblanc shook his head.

"If we get enough personnel involved, we might just get him. The ranch has a drone and they're sending it up now. They are better equipped than the police are, it seems. Surely he can't have fled that far by now."

"I hope you're right."

One of the police officers hurried out from the main building, and Leblanc stopped him.

"What's happening?" he asked.

"We've got some of the ranch hands searching near the buildings, but we haven't found any sign of him. The manager is organizing for a few of the wranglers to go out in the SUVs and take a look on the roads surrounding the ranch. They're going to take the drone with them and send it up if they see any signs. You want to go out and check the roads?"

"Yes," Katie said, glad to be able to take action at last, instead of directing people from the site of the attack.

Leblanc nodded, then spoke into the radio.

"The police are setting up roadblocks on all the major highways in case he's running further out. The cowboys are also going to take a couple of horses and patrol the ranch's perimeter."

With the interior and exterior being checked, Katie knew they had the best possible chance of finding the killer.

She rushed around to the garage at the back of the ranch and climbed into the driver's seat of a ranch vehicle. Leblanc got into the passenger seat, and they roared down the drive.

"There are a couple of side roads he could have used as escape routes. If he's got a car parked, we might find his tracks. Or even better, the car itself."

"I hope you're right," Katie said.

The snow was thick on the ground, so the SUV's tires left deep tracks as they moved along the road. Katie drove for a minute over the soft, crunchy surface, then swerved off the main road onto a side road that bordered the southern part of the ranch.

Scanning the darkness for any sign of their quarry, they crested a small hill and traveled along the side of a wide valley. The headlights flashed against the snow, throwing shadows against the drifts that made her heart quicken every time, as they looked like a crouching man.

Leblanc shone the spotlight from the window as they passed a forested area, scanning the bushes and trees.

But as they drove, they saw nothing. The snow was undisturbed. No footprints, no tire tracks.

She turned again and headed around the ranch's lower border, noticing the helicopter circling nearby.

"Surely he can't have escaped this search?" Leblanc sounded incredulous.

"He had two big advantages. Speed and surprise," Katie said. "It took us a while to get organized and he clearly had an escape route planned."

She swallowed a sigh at the thought of their quarry vanishing into the snowy night. She didn't want to give up on him, but she knew they had to be realistic. They couldn't stay out until dawn in this weather if he was already long gone. Nor could they ask the police and ranch hands to pursue a futile exercise.

Farther along the road, they passed the turn off that led to the ranch owner's house. She pulled up to the next intersection and stopped. Leblanc looked around again.

"There's been no sign of him. The snow on these roads is undisturbed. Wherever he went, it wasn't here."

"I think he planned this out. He had an escape route in mind and he took it, fast," Katie said. "Most likely he crossed through the woods to cover his tracks, and then used a snowmobile to get clear of the area. Or he could have hidden a car in the back roads on the other side of the woods."

Leblanc nodded grimly as they turned back up the driveway.

"We could use the map again and look at where he might strike next," Leblanc suggested. "There was a definite pattern visible last time and it was correct. That's one thing we have, at least."

"We do," Katie said gratefully. "You were right. You predicted he would target this ranch and it's exactly the one he chose."

"If he tried to strike here and failed, he might not try again, but rather move on to the next location. So we need to work out what it might be."

"That's a good idea," Katie said.

They headed up the driveway, parked in the garage, and climbed out of the car. Then they both headed into Leblanc's chalet. The room was warm and cozy, but Katie checked carefully around before she sat down, knowing that in the rush, Leblanc had left it unlocked. Her skin still prickled with adrenaline as she remembered the suddenness of that terrifying attack.

Once she was sure the room was clear, Leblanc took out the map and unfolded it and they both stared down.

"Here. This one. Silver Creek. It's twenty miles to the north. It fits in perfectly with the rough pattern he's following."

Katie peered down at the map. Now that the adrenaline of the chase was ebbing, her eyes felt tired and dry and she realized how exhausted she was after the long day and sleepless night. But they needed to be on site at Silver Creek next, in case their presence could help to prevent the next death.

"I'll call ahead to Silver Creek, to put them on alert and get them prepared," Katie said. "As soon as the police are finished here, we must tell them. I know they're thinly stretched this far north, but they might be able to put a couple of officers on site."

Quickly, Katie made the call to Silver Creek.

The manager there sounded alert and worried when he answered.

"There's a chance, based on the killer's pattern, that he might be targeting your ranch next. Please stay alert," Katie told him.

"I will tell my team now. What else can we do?" the manager asked.

"My partner and I would like to be on site at your ranch so that we're in the area."

"That will be possible. Absolutely. We have a few rooms prepared. Please, come through immediately. I'll be waiting at the main building," the manager said.

The line went dead, and Katie turned to Leblanc.

“I don’t know what we can do if he changes his tactics again. But we have to try and keep ahead of him. If we can prevent another death, we’re winning.”

Her fingers touched the rip in her jacket, feeling the shredded fabric where the knife had sliced through.

"I hope he continues with his pattern, and doesn’t change things up completely," Leblanc said.

"You were right about this ranch. And he only changed things by choosing a different time. Not a different place," Katie said, wondering what this meant about the way this killer was planning his crimes.

Katie headed back to her chalet to pack her things, trying to ignore the rising feeling of dread inside her as she thought about what she knew and could predict.

The killer had been frustrated and he hadn't achieved what he had come for, thanks to her fighting back. Plus, by now, he would certainly have seen the police and heard the helicopter and know that they were starting to close in on him.

Based on her knowledge of serial killers, Katie was sure this would not put him off for long. It would mean he would have to temporarily regroup. She didn’t think he would try again tonight. Not when it was clear the area was on high alert and tightly locked down. Instead, he would lay low and work out a new plan. But she had no doubt he would strike soon.

They had bought a few hours of safety. But from dawn tomorrow, Katie knew, the risk would redouble as he looked for the first opportunity to murder again.

CHAPTER TWENTY TWO

Katie sat bolt upright in bed, breathing rapidly, jerked from a nightmare she couldn't remember, but which left her with a chilly sense of dread.

The plush bedroom was quiet. Muted light, reflected off snow, filtered in through the window drapes. Climbing out of bed and walking across the carpeted floor, she stared out at the unfamiliar view from the window of the main lodge at Silver Creek. She felt grateful she'd managed to get a couple of hours of sleep, but deeply worried about what the killer might have been planning in the quiet small hours.

There was no sign of anyone outside. At this early hour, the ranch looked quiet and peaceful.

But it was a big ranch. Thousands of acres. It chilled her to think that he was preparing for his next strike, hidden away in the vastness.

She went back to the bed and checked the time on her cell phone. It was quarter to seven in the morning. Time to get up and plan the day. Quickly, she scrambled into her clothes and headed out. Her room was on the second floor of the ranch, and as soon as she stepped into the corridor, she smelled coffee and heard the chink of cutlery from the dining room below.

She hurried down the stairs, arriving in the dining room at the same time as a red-eyed Leblanc. He too looked exhausted after the events of last night, and she was sure he hadn't slept either.

"At least the rest of the night was quiet," Leblanc said in a low voice as they sat at a corner table.

"I expected that. But he's speeding up his interval, and if I'm reading him right, he'll look to strike again today," Katie muttered back.

At that moment, the ranch manager who'd welcomed them and shown them to their rooms in the early hours, arrived with a jug of coffee. He, too, looked short on sleep, but gave them a brisk smile.

"Morning, detectives. Thank you for helping to keep us safe. We've notified all guests this morning already and have placed some of our staff in pairs, on the routes to the walkways, to make sure nobody goes out on their own. As you can imagine, there's some panic." He grimaced.

"I'm sorry about the panic. That's inevitable, I guess. But for now, the key is to be prepared and be vigilant," Leblanc said.

"We have a security team, and some of us will be armed. When the ranch hands aren't busy with the horses and cattle, they will patrol within the grounds. There's only one road leading into and out of here. We'll also check around the perimeter of the ranch," he said.

"That's all sounding good," Katie said.

At that moment, her phone rang.

It was Scott on the line, and her heart quickened as she saw his number. Surely the killer could not have struck in a different location? She dreaded he was calling to tell them about another victim.

Even if he wasn't, Katie knew that dire pressure must be bearing down on the task force boss.

"Morning," he said. As she'd expected, he sounded tired and stressed. Guilt twisted inside her that they hadn't gotten further with the case. If only she had managed to grab her attacker and hold him, instead of allowing him to get away.

"Morning, Scott. How's it going?" she asked.

"Not very well. There's more pressure on us now. I've got a meeting with the Montana state governor in an hour. Anyway, that's not why I'm calling. I got your update last night. I can't believe you were targeted. Are you sure you're okay?"

"Yes, I wasn't hurt at all. My coat was slashed, but that was all."

"Do you think he knew you were law enforcement? Is that why he struck?" Scott said, worried.

Katie considered the question carefully.

"No. I don't think he had any idea. I think he was on the lookout for a guest going to or from the main chalet, and he thought I was one of them. When I fought back, he was surprised. And when I started yelling, and Leblanc rushed over, he ran."

"Any signs so far today?"

"Nothing yet, but we're in the place where he should strike again, based on his geographical pattern," she said. "He's been changing things up, though. Attacking at night was a change. So he might choose a different ranch but my feeling will be that he'll stick to this area, because he will have scoped out the escape routes."

"I hope you catch him before another attack," Scott said. "In the meantime, I've had the rest of the team working through the night, looking through news reports from the area and calling the ranches to try and build up a profile of who this guy might be."

"What have you found?" Katie asked, feeling an odd sense of urgency.

"There's a property speculator who's been working the area recently. He's been buying up ranches from people who are elderly, broke, looking to sell, or feeling financial pressure. Paying bottom dollar for them and then selling them on to the wealthy. You might have heard something about it?"

Katie nodded. "Yes. One of the ranch managers did mention that the big ranches had acquired more land," she said.

"He uses the tactics I'm sure you've heard about. Fear, uncertainty, doubt. He tells them values are plummeting. He emphasizes the lack of safety in the area and that it's going to the dogs. Then, when he has enough land, he contacts one of the mega-wealthy ranchers to buy it up for a good price."

"That's very disturbing. He's doing everything he can to drive down values?" Katie asked. She glanced at Leblanc and saw he was on the same page as her. They both understood exactly where this agent might be going with these tactics.

Nothing drove property values down like violent crime. Having a greedy speculator keen to acquire land for bottom dollar was certainly a coincidence.

"There's more," Scott added. "He's just put in an offer to acquire a large portion of Caribou Wilderness Resort. That's where the last murder occurred."

"We need to find this man urgently. What's his name?" Katie asked.

"His name's Trevor Downey and he's based in Great Falls."

Glancing at the map, Katie saw that was an hour's drive away.

"We'll be on our way immediately," she said, jumping up from her chair and grabbing her car keys.

*

An hour later, after driving at top speed along the icy roads, Katie and Leblanc pulled up outside Trevor Downey's offices in Great Falls.

Katie understood the mindset of people like Trevor Downey. Preying on innocent and vulnerable people, using lies and bullying tactics, was a slippery slope and it could easily have escalated. After all there were only limited numbers of elderly or broke folk who were willing to sell up at a low price. Once they'd been targeted, an unethical and greedy man who also happened to be a psychopath, would need to find more ways to pressure the market in his favor.

The buildings on the side road were classic Montana architecture and the townhouse where Trevor's offices were located was a charming, double-story, timber building with a large wrap-around porch.

They climbed out of the car and headed over to the building.

Inside, Katie could see an assistant at work in a brightly lit front office. She tapped on the door before pushing it open.

The young woman looked up expectantly.

"Can I help you?" she asked.

"Good morning. Agent Winter and Detective Leblanc. We need to speak to Mr. Downey," Katie said, wasting no time.

The receptionist's eyes widened.

"He's not here. He's out on a site inspection," she said hesitantly.

"Can you tell us when he'll be back?" Katie asked.

"He's not coming back into the office today at all. I guess we can expect him back this evening."

"Where's his home address?"

She hesitated. "I - I don't know if I'm allowed to disclose that? I'd rather he gave you that information as I might get into trouble. But he's not at home now, that I do know."

"Where is he now? This is a federal murder investigation so you are obliged to tell us," Leblanc pressured her.

"He's out on a site inspection of one of the properties we're interested in acquiring," she said.

"Can you give us the address?" Katie asked.

Again, she hesitated, but Katie's glare convinced her.

"It's the Old Thomson Farm. It's a half-hour's drive away from here, on Bootlegger Trail road, going north."

"Thank you. We'll take a business card, if you don't mind," Katie said, noticing a pile of them on the desk. Now they had his cellphone number, too.

They were hot on the trail of a man who seemed willing to use any tactics to grab up property at a low price.

She hoped they could catch up with Trevor Downey fast.

CHAPTER TWENTY THREE

Leblanc was feeling impatient and stressed as they turned into the road where the Old Thomson Farm was located. The drive had given him a chance to think, and what he'd been thinking was that Katie had taken a totally unnecessary risk last night. How could he work with her as a trusted partner, when she decided to go off on midnight walks on her own?

Anger and guilt warred for precedence as the disaster with Cecile loomed in his mind again. He was grateful for the distraction when the farm finally came in sight.

He'd been expecting a dilapidated place, ripe for the picking, but to his surprise the small ranch seemed to be well cared for.

The fence was in good condition, and healthy cattle were pulling hay from racks in the snowy field. The house was painted a pristine white, with a small but well tended garden.

Outside the front door they saw an enormous SUV was parked intimidatingly close to the house.

Stopping behind it, Leblanc climbed out and walked to the house with Katie. He prepared himself for the confrontation ahead, knowing it was likely this speculator would be devious and a liar. He had no doubt at all that he would also be a bully.

Katie rang the doorbell, and a moment later, a gray-haired woman hurried to the door. She looked upset and rattled.

"Is Trevor Downey here? We're investigating a series of murders and need to speak to him," Leblanc said, flashing his badge.

"Mr. Downey?" She stared at them in shock, as if wondering what on earth was going on. "Yes, yes he's here at the moment. But we're busy with him - er - I guess you can come in."

The woman stood aside, looking flustered. They stepped into the neat farmhouse. As soon as they were inside, Leblanc could hear raised voices coming from the door down the passage. Hurrying toward them, he found himself in a small lounge. There, a gray-haired man was sitting in a floral-upholstered chair. A wide-shouldered, domineering man was standing in front of him and leaning threateningly into his space.

When Leblanc and Katie walked in, the man swung around to face them. He was wearing a thick, dark, cashmere coat and designer clothing. He had a bullying demeanor and an arrogant expression on his face.

Leblanc glanced immediately at Katie who raised her eyebrows ever so slightly in confirmation. That meant this man did fit the physical parameters of her attacker last night, and was in the ballpark for height and weight. But being warmly wrapped up, no scrapes or bruises would be obvious, if he had incurred any in the brief struggle.

Leblanc noted that his face changed, briefly tautening in apprehension as he stared at them. But he didn't know if that was because he recognized Katie, or simply because two people who were very clearly law enforcement had arrived at the house where he was pressuring a buyer.

"Mr. Downey, these detectives are here to see you," the gray-haired woman said timidly.

Trevor now looked astounded.

"Me? What's this? Why are you here?" he demanded.

"Mr. Downey, is it?" Leblanc asked. He could see the man had a calculating, ruthless look in his eyes.

Trevor didn't answer but just stared them down.

"We're investigating a series of murders which are centered on this area. We need to ask you some questions," Leblanc began.

"Have I done something wrong? If not, then I guess I'm not your man. Do you have a warrant? If not you can make an appointment to see me. I have a business to run and I can't afford to be wasting time here answering your questions," he said.

Leblanc saw immediately he was both defensive and aggressive. He didn't know if this was his natural attitude or if it was exacerbated by guilt.

"This is a federal investigation," Leblanc insisted.

"I'm not responsible for any murders," Trevor Downey said, shaking his head with an arrogant smile. "I genuinely don't understand why you are here. If there have been murders, you should be hunting for the killer and not harassing local businessmen."

"We believe that you're involved in an ongoing land speculation scheme in the area. What we want to know is how you're going about it," Leblanc said. "We know you're using underhanded tactics to acquire properties, including intimidation, bullying, and misrepresenting the facts. And unfortunately for you, there have been murders in the area where you've been working, so we need to question you immediately."

He heard both the ranch owners gasp at this bombshell. Whatever else happened, Leblanc hoped that he'd blown Downey out of the water and stopped him from intimidating them into selling.

"I do not have to explain myself to you," he said, taking a threatening step toward them.

"You are obstructing justice if you refuse to answer questions related to a murder investigation," Katie said, standing her ground.

"Where were you yesterday? What were your movements in the morning, and late at night?" Leblanc pressured him.

"None of your damned business!" the man said, taking another step.

"I'll ask you again. Where were you yesterday?" Leblanc said. Now it was his turn to stare his opponent down.

"My business is my own affair. You have no right to harass me like this."

Leblanc took a step closer to him. "You do realize that by evading the questions, you're setting yourself up to look guilty?"

Trevor Downey's eyes narrowed. "That's ridiculous. I'm not responsible for any murders. I'm a businessman, trying to make an honest living."

"The evidence shows otherwise," Leblanc said.

"You have no evidence against me," he replied. "Not for anything I've done."

The gray-haired ranch owner cleared his throat.

"Actually, I think he might have been lying to us just now. He said we'd better sell to him as the state is going to run a gas pipeline through our property and it will be worthless after that. I've never heard of such thing but he said he'd personally spoken to the senator responsible. And he then said that when the pipeline comes, crime and pollution will spike."

Trevor glared at him. Leblanc saw Katie raise her eyebrows, noting this evidence.

"I know that you bought the farm a few miles to the north, and that they went through a terrible time before they sold," the gray-haired woman added accusingly. "They had a fire that burned down their barn with all the winter hay inside. And their water supply was cut off numerous times due to broken pipes," she added. "You just told my husband that we'd better be careful or the same thing will happen to us."

Leblanc glared at Trevor, noticing his face had now turned a deep, boiling red.

"It happened to them because they're idiots who don't know how to run a farm," he said, his voice booming.

"Have you used brute force to intimidate people into selling to you? How much further would you take things?" Katie asked. Leblanc could see she was aiming to pressurize him into an explosion.

"I have no idea what you're talking about," Trevor blustered. "As I said, I don't have to tell you anything more. I'm not responsible for any murders," he said, his voice rising.

"We'll decide that, not you. You're coming into the police department with us now," Leblanc said.

"No, I'm not! I don't have to answer your questions," he bellowed.

"You are obstructing the course of justice in an investigation into an ongoing series of murders. You have no choice. You're coming in with us," Leblanc insisted.

"You can't arrest me. I haven't done anything," he shouted.

"We aren't arresting you. We're just asking you to accompany us to the station. You can give us your version of events there."

"I don't even have to do that. I have a right to protect my privacy," he snarled.

"No, you don't. Your privacy ends where the investigation begins. You will accompany us now," Katie stressed.

Leblanc was beginning to realize that Trevor wasn't just being obstructive. He was terrified of being brought in. His blustered attempts at intimidation were a last-ditch effort to avoid this.

"I have nothing to say to you." The words were uttered through gritted teeth.

Leblanc was convinced now that he was hiding something. Undoubtedly this man was involved in something criminal. Now, all that remained was to find out if he'd gone as far as murder.

"If you won't cooperate, then we'll do things the hard way," Leblanc said, grabbing his arm. "I think we've got enough to hold you until we can look into these matters more thoroughly. You're being detained on suspicion of racketeering and murder. "We're taking you to the Great Falls police department for questioning. You're now a suspect. So you'd better start talking soon," he stressed.

Trevor's eyes widened and he tried to yank his arm away, but Leblanc was too quick and held on. Katie grabbed his other arm, and they got the cuffs around his wrists.

In a moment, Leblanc was hustling the furious, yelling property speculator to the car.

*

In the harsh light of the police interview room, an hour later, Trevor Downey didn't look as brashly confident anymore.

Leblanc strolled into the room, taking his time.

"I believe the owners of Old Thomson Farm are going to be laying charges of harassment and intimidation against you. And their neighbors are going to be looking into the damage that was done to their property. We're going to see if your vehicle was in the area at the time of the fire, or on the nights when the pipes were broken. There are highway cameras along the route, and there's a camera heading into town that you would have passed by. You're in serious trouble if we find you were there when those events took place."

Trevor stared back at him through narrowed eyes. Leblanc could see he was sweating.

"I need to know where you were. Because otherwise, we're going to add murder to the list of charges. And based on what we have gathered already in such a short time, there probably isn't a jury who will believe your version."

Trevor wiped a trickle of sweat from his temple.

"I - I was in a confidential meeting the whole of yesterday. With someone from the Bureau of Land Management."

Feeling a thud of disappointment at this potential alibi, Leblanc pressed on.

"His name? Don't worry about getting people into trouble. At this stage, it's them or you."

"Here." Trevor produced a business card from his pocket. "This - this could get me into a lot of trouble," he insisted.

"And last night?"

"I was here in Great Falls. Um, with someone from the Montana Land Board."

Leblanc raised his eyebrows. He could imagine the reasons for that meeting.

"I took them to dinner. I can show you the restaurant booking, and they will confirm we were there. We left at about eleven."

"All right," Leblanc said. "If these check out, you won't be facing murder charges. But you're still under arrest for the lesser charges. The local police department will be handling the case."

He left the interview room feeling deflated.

They had captured and charged a racketeer who had inflicted malicious harm on many property owners.

But they hadn't yet captured the killer, and as Katie had explained, he'd be looking to speed up his cycle now. With every moment that passed, Leblanc expected to get the call he dreaded, that the man had struck again.

He jumped as, from his pocket, his phone began to ring.

CHAPTER TWENTY FOUR

M couldn't believe it. He was horrified.

Mediocre. Mess-up.

What had happened last night? Up until that time he'd considered himself to be strong, invulnerable, fast enough to get the jump on any of his victims. Especially since he'd chosen them so carefully.

And then, out of nowhere, the woman last night had fought back with a speed and viciousness that had astounded him.

She'd managed to hurt him. He could easily have dropped his knife, and it had been sheer luck he'd managed to hold it. And after that he'd been on the defensive. He'd had to run when her cries had alerted someone else. He'd never thought she would have time to scream, not with her throat ripped open, the way it should have been.

He had been forced to flee like a coward, to abandon his carefully prepared kill. He had sacrificed the revenge he was craving.

It had been one of the worst moments of his life.

Frantic with confusion, he paced up and down inside his small bedroom, remembering.

He'd known he had to get away, fast. At least he'd managed to stay calm enough to follow his plan. He'd even swept his tracks before he entered the woods, so that they wouldn't see which way he'd gone once he was in the trees. But the clamor behind him, the lights, the people that he'd seen milling around and heading out as he watched from the safety of the hilltop before bolting for his hidden car – they all presented a threat that he'd only just escaped.

All morning, faintly, he'd thought he had heard the thrum of helicopter blades and he feared they were hunting him. Closing in. They wanted to stop him from his quest for justice, that he knew.

He'd been prepared to kill again and make up for the time he'd lost, and he'd set out at first light, headed toward the highway, ready to do the deed. But then, to his shame, he'd lost his nerve. Fearing they would be waiting for him there, he had decided he couldn't bear to be trapped like that.

What had happened? Had he suddenly weakened? Was he now incapable of doing what he needed to?

And then, a sudden thought came to him.

Of course!

The woman must have been a plainclothes policeman.

Why couldn't he have realized before? It made perfect sense. No wonder she'd been so strong, so fast.

She had attacked him exactly as if she had been a trained fighter. No ordinary civilian could have avoided his attack, ducked and moved as she had done. He had experience in that. He'd done a couple of years in the army in his early twenties, before he'd fought with one of his peers, hurt him badly, and ended up being dishonorably discharged. None of it had been fair. None of his life had been fair at all, which was why he needed to do what he was busy with now.

His hand was still smarting and his head was pounding. He wondered if she'd hit him hard enough to crack a rib.

He shook his head. What a stupid thought. He didn't have lasting damage. It was just the cold he was feeling.

The thought calmed him.

He would regroup, but this time, would learn from his mistake. Of course he would try again. It was his mission now. But this time he would be more prepared. He wouldn't fall for their tricks, but would be more vigilant and careful. He would not let them catch him.

But he needed to change the way he operated, he mused. If they were planting people to entrap him, it meant they were ready for him.

He couldn't risk attacking another plainclothes officer again. The next time he might not get away.

M mused over this, leaning on the wooden windowsill and staring out at the snow. He would have to make absolutely sure that his target was who he thought they were. So he couldn't risk going down to the ranch itself in future. That had been a stupid move, reckless and ill-advised. But he would learn from his mistakes.

He would be sure, this time, to pick someone who wouldn't pose a threat to him. It would be possible to find that person, he knew it. It would just take more patience than before. He would make sure that his escape route was well mapped out, and would remain calm.

He was going to stay a step ahead of him and make sure that they lagged far behind. He'd done it before and could do it again. They had no idea who he was, that he was sure of.

Confidence surged inside him. Once again he was in control.

No one messed with M and got away with it.

Nodding in satisfaction, he put on a different set of clothing, knowing they'd be alert for the snow camouflage he had worn last night.

He headed out, taking his truck, even though he also had the choice of a snowmobile. But for this next outing, a truck would be better for the roads in the area he was planning to hit. Climbing inside, he drove carefully, keeping to the speed limit, obeying all the traffic laws and making sure not to draw attention to himself. By the time he reached the main intersection, he was calmer.

He hesitated. Straight, left or right? There were three options open to him to get where he needed to be. It was a site he'd planned to use in a few days' time, but he was jumping ahead, making sure he outpaced his enemies. He needed to choose a route where the police wouldn't be waiting.

M knew the area well. He was very familiar with the hiding places, and there were many of them, where a car could pull off the road and be invisible within a few seconds.

Left would work best. Nodding in satisfaction, he powered along the snowy road, looking for the turnoff he needed.

There it was, up ahead. After checking there were no other cars around, he pulled quickly off the road. He killed the lights and waited, watching.

He was still angry at his mistake. This time, he was determined to be ready for any trick they might try. First and foremost, he needed to make sure he hadn't been followed or noticed.

He watched a minute flick by on the car clock. Patiently, he waited for one more to pass before deciding it was safe. He climbed out. Dense forest stretched out around him on all sides, the trees thick with snow.

He shivered, feeling the cold biting through his clothing as he zipped up the parka and pulled his hat down low on his forehead. Before leaving the car, he made sure he had his binoculars in their case and the knife in his pocket.

It was too cold to stand around, so he picked his way down the long, snowy embankment. Sure enough, a long, narrow track led off through the trees.

M grinned. If anyone else found this, they would think it was a deer trail. It was covered with debris, leaves and branches, which would obscure his footprints.

He was in no hurry. He knew he would be able to find several good lookout points along the way.

The first one he came to, high on the hill, was a windfall, a tree that had fallen over, leaving a gap between the snow on the ground and the sky overhead. If he crouched down, he would be entirely concealed.

It was perfect. It reminded him of the places he used to play as a child, making tunnels in the snow. He edged forward to the gap, checked to make sure no one was around, and then he wriggled closer.

Pausing, he listened for a moment, but couldn't hear anything.

Only silence.

The snow was deep, and the cold seeped through his clothing.

M raised his binoculars and grinned.

Ahead of him, he had a perfect view of the wooden chalets, and the criss-crossed paths leading away from them. He could see a couple of people, small but clear figures, strolling along the paths.

He watched for what felt like a long time, immersed in the scene before him as he noted the comings and goings, the way the people moved, the way they interacted with each other.

Wealthy, arrogant people. How clearly he remembered their sneers and suspicion. The accusations they'd brought against him, their derogatory comments. The scorn they had showed by not understanding what his needs were. No, they hadn't cared about him at all. Only about themselves.

As he watched, he felt the joy of anticipation build inside him. They had tried to make him fear them, but he would not be defeated. He would not let them stop him.

They thought they could arrest him, entrap him. They thought they could control him. But he would not be controlled. He would not let them take away his right to justice.

It was time to kill again.

CHAPTER TWENTY FIVE

Katie saw Leblanc stomp out of the police department's interview room as she emerged from the back office. He was glowering and looked frustrated.

"What happened?" she asked in concern, rushing to meet him at the door. "Did you not get a confession from him? Is he still refusing to talk to you? I knew we should have gone in together."

He'd opted to interview Trevor alone to start with, while she drew up the charges with the local detectives. Now, she worried that the crooked speculator had redoubled his defenses and was obstructing them again.

Clearly in a terrible mood, Leblanc glowered at her.

"There was no confession to be had. He had an alibi. He was busy doing more of the same. Bribery, intimidation, corruption. I have all the details. He's as corrupt as can be, but he's not our man."

"Oh, no." That was a huge blow. Everything about Trevor had indicated he was a likely suspect.

"Oh, yes," Leblanc confirmed glumly.

"Are you sure?" Katie asked.

"I'll be sure as soon as I've checked out the details he's given me," Leblanc snapped. He was clearly triggered by what she'd inadvertently said earlier, because then he added, "If he had been guilty, I would have gotten a confession, you know. I can't believe you think I would be incompetent!"

Katie turned to face him. He was glaring at her like she was a worm to be squashed under his shoe. Clearly he'd been invested in this outcome and was now bitterly disappointed.

"I wasn't saying that! I was saying two of us might have made a difference."

"Maybe that should have occurred to you earlier," Leblanc snapped, and now she realized with a shock what lay behind his anger. "Because you nearly got yourself killed by going off alone last night! I seriously can't believe you did anything so irresponsible!"

"What?" Katie felt enraged by his words. Was he implying she was not a responsible person?

"I don't think that's fair," she said angrily. "I was planning to go to the ranch house. Not for a walk. I just turned the wrong way."

Leblanc said coldly. "I think you're lucky to be alive, but you shouldn't have been out there at all."

"What? If I hadn't been, he would have waited for someone else!" she protested.

But Leblanc was unstoppable as he forged ahead with what Katie knew was an extremely unfair attack.

"You need to realize you're part of a team. Not some renegade acting on her own. You should have checked in with me before going anywhere. You need to start proving you're a team player. Do you not understand what a disaster it would have been if he had killed you, or you'd been badly injured?"

Katie's fury burst into flames.

"All I did was go for a walk and turn the wrong way. You have no idea why I couldn't sleep or why I needed to go and find a book. I wasn't heading out into the wilderness! The fact he was there, was a complete shock. And you should stop trying to control all my thoughts and actions."

"I'm not trying to control anything," Leblanc stated heavily. "I'm just pointing out that you are the one who should be controlling them yourself."

Katie just stood there and stared at him. Stunned. Angry. She had a thousand things to say, but she couldn't get a word out. She was fuming too much to speak. To argue. She refused to be trapped in this conversation. She wasn't going to defend herself or let him bait her into unpleasantness.

"All right, then," she spat at him. Not a great comeback. It wasn't what she had planned to say.

He glared at her.

Suddenly, the tension between them was unbearable. Katie felt as if she was walking through a minefield. Every step she took she expected to step on something that would explode under her feet.

"I'm going to take another look at that map," she said finally. "Then I might go for a drive. I'll see you later."

Without waiting for a reply, she turned on her heel and walked away.

Still seething, Katie headed outside and climbed into the car. She started it up and set off, accelerating down the snowy street. She had no idea where she would go next, but she knew she needed to be away from there. Leblanc's words had hit her like a sucker punch to the gut.

She'd triggered him by doubting his abilities, she knew that, but why did he have to retaliate with such hurtfully accurate criticism?

Katie had been reckless in walking on her own when a serial killer had targeted that location. Did she wrongly think she was immortal? Invulnerable? Was she letting the team down with self-destructive behavior? Those were hard truths to consider, but she had to admit she'd made a terrible mistake and he'd called her out on it.

At this moment, she felt desperate to talk to someone, and it pained her once again that she had a nonexistent relationship with her mother. Imagine being able to pick up the phone and call her? Imagine that closeness.

Mothers would sympathize.

Except her mother hadn't. At a time when Katie had been at her most vulnerable, she'd turned her back on her and she'd been confronted with silence, the worst weapon of all.

Katie turned right at the stop street. She felt calmer now that she was driving.

She didn't have a mother she could confide in, but perhaps her thoughts were leading her in the direction she needed to go. Closeness was on her mind.

The killer had to be closer to the picture than they'd been thinking. That idea had seemed to come out of nowhere, but maybe it was a hint she was meant to notice.

In their desire to track him down they had widened the search. But maybe it was time to spiral back in, and to look once again at who was closely involved with the area and with all the ranches. Who was a troublemaker in the local area. He had to have local knowledge.

If only she could ask the right questions, and think along the right lines, she could pinpoint him. She felt sure of it.

She felt pleased she'd had that insight that reminded her to focus on the affected area, that represented his hunting ground.

And at that moment, her phone rang.

It was Leblanc. Her blood pressure spiked as she saw his name on the screen. Had he thought of a few more insults? Sighing, knowing she had to, she took the call.

As soon as she answered, she knew he was still in a bad mood.

"I need you to come back," he snapped. "Why the hell must you run away every time there's a problem?"

Katie closed her eyes briefly. She felt the frustration of their earlier conversation bubble up again. Why did he have to be like that? He was so good at his job. But he knew how to make her feel like she was incompetent.

At this time, she knew she needed to be rational.

""I'm not running away," she said quietly. "I'm on my way back. What's happened?"

"The cops here looked back over the department's records in case there were any suspects that might fit the description." Leblanc now sounded haughtily pleased with himself.

"And were there?" she asked.

"There's one guy who's a known doomsday prepper. He's been in trouble with them numerous times in the past few years. Guns, drugs, and bribing the police. He's a dangerous guy. Erratic. Very aggressive. He's given them big problems in the past few years. He's threatened ranch owners. Threatened guests. He attacked a guest during a road rage incident. And a ranch owner, during a discussion about boundary lines."

Katie felt fresh hope. "So, what's his name?"

"Virgil Harvey," Leblanc said. "I have his exact location. He lives out in the wilderness. But his house is very central to all the affected ranches so far. It's not more than a couple of hours' drive from any of them."

The clouds of earlier had lifted somewhat, and the sun was warming the air. It was freezing outside, but Katie felt a growing anticipation race through her veins.

"That seems like a promising lead," she agreed.

No matter if she and her partner were on speaking terms or not, this new suspect was slap bang in the red zone where he would have easy access to every ranch that had been hit.

"Glad you're finally taking me seriously."

Katie was confused by his tone. Was that sarcasm or aggression?

Still, she kept her focus on the lead, remembering they had a killer to catch.

"I'll be there in five minutes. See you outside," she said, and hung up.

CHAPTER TWENTY SIX

"Honey, wait!"

Christine Parr yelled ahead to her husband as she floundered through the snow. Her hips were killing her. This cross-country skiing had seemed far more fun in theory, than it was in real, freezing life. It was icy cold, the snow was rough and compacted, and she was exhausted.

Maybe thirty years ago this would have counted as fun. But not now.

"Wait for what?" Evan called from ahead.

He was forging through the snow at a tireless pace.

"Wait for me, honey!" she cried out once more, her breath billowing out in front of her.

She'd have been much better off staying inside and playing card games by the fire.

"I'm slowing up," he replied, and finally his inexorable progress stopped.

He turned and waited for her, a little smile on his face. "You're not going to give up, are you?" he asked.

"Of course not," she replied, panting hard. "I'm just taking a moment. I need to breathe."

"Oh, for goodness sake, come on," he said, his voice getting agitated. "Let's just keep going."

"I can't," she said, gasping. "I'm so tired."

"You're just not used to exercise," he said, thumping her on the back. "It'll come. Keep going. You'll feel much better once we're on the downhill."

"That's what you said last time." She groaned. "There's never a downhill. I'm going to take a rest."

She paused on the trail, panting. Her breath clouded the air, and she shook her head to try and stop her ears from aching.

"We're so close," he said. "It's only a little way to the top of the ridge. You can see the top of the mountain from up there. We should be able to see the whole valley. You know what that means? We'll be able to see the next ranch."

He didn't wait, though. He just got up and left her there, still puffing and struggling.

She knew she should just get up, go after him, and keep moving. But she was bone weary, and her muscles were aching.

"I have to have a rest," she called after him.

But he didn't even turn around.

With a sigh, she stepped forward again.

"Christine, come on," he urged. "We're so close now."

And then he cried out, real pain in his voice, and dropped to the ground in front of her.

"What is it?" Anxiously, she made slow progress toward him. What had happened?

"It's my knee," Evan groaned, clutching it. "I was doing so well but it just gave out on me. This is the same injury I had in my thirties. Come back to bite me at the worst time."

"Oh, what a shame," she said, in real sympathy. "Here, let me look at it. Perhaps we can wrap it with something?"

"No." He shook his head. "I don't want you to help. Just stay there, I'll be—"

But he couldn't finish his sentence. He groaned again and then collapsed onto the snow.

"Is it very bad?" she asked, feeling anxious now, while he grimaced with pain.

"I can't walk on it. I could try, but it will probably make it worse." He tried to stand and shook his head in defeat, sinking to the ground again.

"Can we call for help?"

Christine realized she hadn't brought her phone with her. Evan had his.

He pulled it from his pocket and fumbled with the keys.

"There's no signal here," he said. "Not on my network. Your phone picks up more signal on this ranch. But you don't have yours with you, do you?" He stared at her accusingly.

"No, I'm so sorry. I had no idea we'd need it. But I'll go back down and call for a snowmobile, or something. Then I'll come back here with them. The lodge can drive you straight to a doctor, or even to the hospital."

"Yeah," Evan said reluctantly. "I guess we'll have to do that. Be quick, though. I don't want to wait around in the cold."

Christine was so used to Evan putting his needs ahead of hers that she didn't even notice the unfairness of the situation.

"I will." She turned and started back down the trail, feeling anxious about getting back fast. She glanced back and saw him, still lying in the snow, his face twisted with pain.

"I'll be as quick as I can!" she shouted back to him. "You just stay there."

She felt terrible that she'd forgotten her phone. Self-blame filled her as she forged her way slowly back down the hill.

Hopefully, there would be someone who could come out in a vehicle and attend to him immediately, because she was looking forward to getting out of this cold.

Christine stumbled and caught her breath, reminding herself to be careful. She didn't want to fall and get injured, too. Then where would they be?

As she trudged down the snowy trail, feeling relieved when it joined the main path, she turned her head, feeling sure she had heard a noise behind her.

Was it Evan? Had he managed to get going again on his damaged knee?

She stopped and waited.

"Hello? Evan?" she called into the trees behind her.

The mountain was quiet, apart from the wind that whistled through the trees.

Maybe she was just imagining things, just hearing things. But then she heard it again. This time it was unmistakable. A steady, rustling noise.

"What was that?" she asked out loud.

It sounded like someone was forging their way through the forest towards her. She swallowed nervously. Who was it?

Was it another hiker, even though she hadn't noticed anyone else heading out?

Perhaps it was a deer or a coyote, or something like that. She hoped it wasn't a bear, emerged from hibernation, hungry and aggressive.

Then again, it could just be the wind. She waited, straining her ears, but there was nothing else.

Christine turned and walked on, now more determined than ever to get down. But, as she shifted her weight to take another step, she heard the noise again. She couldn't see anything in the trees. But there was a noise – the noise of someone moving. So they had to be there.

"Hello?" she called out again, feeling suddenly nervous.

This truly wasn't her imagination. There was someone else up there. If she could get their attention, they might be able to call for help.

"Hello?" She strained her eyes in the direction of the noise, but she couldn't see clearly through the snowy trees.

She inched forward cautiously.

"Is there anybody there?"

Christine suddenly felt very alone and vulnerable, out in this icy wilderness.

But then, from behind her, she heard the soft thud-thud of footsteps in the snow. She turned and saw a man approaching. He seemed average height, strong looking.

Was he a ranch hand? He didn't seem to be wearing the uniform that was now familiar to her. And what was he carrying in his hand? It looked - it looked strange. Like some kind of a blade?

"Hi," she said, trying to make her voice sound calm and friendly.

"Hey there," he said, his voice deep. "You lost?"

"No, no. I'm a guest at the ranch. My husband's hurt. He injured his knee. He's back up there and I'm heading down to get help."

"You seemed scared," the man said, frowning.

"I thought I heard something in the woods," she explained.

As Christine looked at him, she started feeling even more nervous. This man was definitely not a ranch employee. He looked too rough. He wasn't in uniform. And that was a seriously sharp looking knife in his hand.

"Who are you?" she asked, edging back a little.

He gazed at her with a strange expression.

"I'm a hunter," he said briefly.

She waited for more, but instead, he muttered to her, "You shouldn't be out here on your own. Have you not heard there have been - incidents?"

There was a weird significance to the way he said that. It chilled her.

"No. We just arrived yesterday and don't know anything. What incidents?" she said, wondering what he meant.

He grasped her arm.

"Come with me," he said.

His grasp was too firm for her to resist. At least she'd be able to move faster with him holding her tight. Christine told herself that she was worrying too much. Why would a criminal be lurking around in the snow? Hoping she was doing the right thing, because he seemed a little strange, Christine walked alongside him, heading for the forested track ahead, trying not to think about the knife he carried in his hand.

CHAPTER TWENTY SEVEN

Leblanc felt irritated beyond belief with Katie as they sped along the highway, heading for the location of their newest suspect.

Why, oh why, did Katie manage to press his buttons so effectively? She was literally maddening! He hadn't meant to lose his temper but something about the way she'd said what she did, had made him feel inadequate. She'd implied that he was incapable of getting a confession from a suspect.

He'd lashed back at her, saying things he regretted, only to feel as if he'd unleashed an explosion!

Now he was doubly angry - at her, and at himself. So there was double the chance he was going to stay mad, and this ride into the wilderness would take place in stony silence.

Hopefully, when they arrived at their destination, they'd get some results, Leblanc thought, derailing his focus from his own annoyance.

The tree-lined road sped by. They were heading into a hilly area, with tracts of white-swathed forest punctuating the bleakness.

At any rate, he thought this was a hopeful lead. The police had been very clear that Virgil Harvey was a troublemaker of note. He'd assaulted police. He had a criminal record for petty theft, violence, and possession of drugs. And he was holed up in this out-of-the-way area that was pretty much equidistant from all the scenes so far. It had to mean something. With any luck, it meant they were now finally heading for the killer's lair.

"It's somewhere here," he said, checking his phone. "But I'm not sure where." He tried to speak calmly, to pretend everything was okay between them and they hadn't just had that huge blow-up.

"This really is like the road to nowhere," she observed, looking from side to side at the uninhabited whiteness, broken only by trees.

"It'll take us to Virgil's place. Or so the police seemed to think."

"I thought the police went out here before?" she asked. "Did they not arrest him at his home? Are we even sure he still lives there? Did you check?"

There was doubt in her voice again and Leblanc gritted his teeth as he realized he was taking it personally, again.

"Last time they came out here was about a year ago, I think. Before that, he got into trouble in a local bar. Maybe he has moved. I'm just going on what I was told." He was sounding defensive again, he knew, but inwardly, Leblanc felt a chill at the unpleasant possibility that this trip would end up being more of a waste of time.

Katie slowed the car.

This was definitely where the coordinates led. They were getting deeper and deeper into the wilderness. Leblanc shivered, his gaze flicking from side to side. It was beautiful, but also eerie.

"Pull off to the right," he said, spotting a rutted track.

They rattled over a cattle grid and drove alongside a rusted wire fence. But beyond, there seemed to be nothing.

Leblanc's heart sank.

The place was empty. It should be a thriving holding, but all he could see was one tumbledown shed.

"It was here," he said, disappointed. "There's the evidence."

"Maybe there's another building nearby," she suggested, as they circled the site. "Otherwise, he must have moved on."

The car bumped over the rough ground. Katie stopped it, and they climbed out.

The wind whistled through Leblanc's coat. It felt a lot colder out here. He walked around the building. The shabby little shack was falling down, the roof sagging.

But something inside caught his eye.

"Hey!" he called.

"What?" Katie shouted back.

"You won't believe this!"

There was a brand-new looking snowmobile parked inside the shack.

Leblanc looked at it incredulously. This entire scenario made no sense. Where was the owner of the snowmobile - hopefully, Virgil himself? Why was this entire place abandoned, with no visible structure that could shelter human life? The shack was a crumbling mass of rotting planks, barely big enough to house a donkey.

"A snowmobile?" Katie sounded just as surprised as she scrunched through the snow toward him.

"He has to be somewhere around here," Leblanc insisted.

"I agree. This snowmobile is an expensive piece of equipment. It's not even dirty. He must have used it. But where is he?" Katie questioned.

Leblanc shook his head. He wished he had an idea. It felt as if this suspect had ridden out here, parked his vehicle, and vanished.

He bent down and crept under the rotting beam, to stand inside the tumbledown shack. It was much darker in here, but on the far side of the shack, Leblanc spied something that intrigued him. In the faint light, it gleamed dully.

"Look at this," he said, pacing over to it curiously.

Set into the ground was a dirty piece of metal. He'd thought it was just old piping. But now he saw it was an actual hatch. In the ground.

It had to lead somewhere. This hatch had to be the reason why the snowmobile was parked outside.

Feeling a sense of total disbelief, because all of this was getting weirder by the moment, Leblanc tugged at the hatch.

It swung open.

Below, going into the ground, he saw a set of metal stairs, leading down to a solid, darkened interior shell.

Katie walked up beside him. Her eyes were wide as she stared down.

"It seems like he's buried a whole container in the ground?" she whispered incredulously. "That's what this looks like."

"He could be down there," Leblanc whispered back.

He rapped sharply on the side of the hatch.

"Police! If you are inside, please come out immediately!"

He waited, but there was no response.

Katie could see she felt as uneasy as he did. This sunken, subterranean refuge smelled weird, and it felt like a trap.

"He might be hiding out down there, or else in the area, watching," she suggested.

"I'll go down," he said. "You stay up here and keep a lookout. I don't trust him not to be hiding out somewhere."

Katie nodded, her hand already on her gun.

"Be careful. I'll take a walk around and see if I can find any tracks, in case he's headed off somewhere else," she said

Leblanc thought he could see dim light filtering from below as he set his foot onto the first stair and crept down as quietly as he could.

He shivered as he descended. The stairway was slippery and narrow. Each stair took time to negotiate, because he was trying to be as quiet as he could. But finally, he reached the second to last stair, and he was far enough down to see inside the space.

The hatch opened into a steel-lined room that was lit by a tiny, flickering light. He heard a hiss. He looked over, startled, and saw that it was a gas lamp.

What on earth was going on here, he wondered, feeling thoroughly spooked as he lowered his foot to take the next step down.

And then, a hand grabbed his leg from behind and yanked him off the stairway.

With a cry, Leblanc crashed down onto the concrete floor, feeling pain lance up through his leg. His head bashed against the metal floor and he briefly saw stars explode in his vision.

To his horror, his gun smashed down on the floor, and he lost his grip on it. It clattered away, falling beyond his reach.

"What the hell are you doing in here?" a voice bellowed.

His attacker came into view, looming over him, looking aggressive and demented, as if he wasn't human at all but rather a strange, wild being who'd been surprised in his lair.

He was a large, solid man in a parka and fur cap, and he was holding an axe.

Leblanc desperately rolled out of the way of the flashing blade. He made a grab for his gun but this madman kicked it away.

"Police!" Leblanc yelled, gritting his teeth in agony, knowing that the word would not be helpful here and might even make things worse.

It didn't have any effect on this madman and nor did it stop his attack.

Leblanc rolled away, trying to scramble to his feet, but the man was on him again, taking a swing at his legs. Fear flared inside him because with this power behind it, an axe blow could be deadly. It might even sever his leg.

He managed to evade most of the blow, but he felt a bone-jarring jolt.

A sharp pain raced up his leg and panic flared inside him, because the axe had found its mark and he had no idea how much damage it had done. Before he could regroup, the axe came whistling down, aiming for his neck.

Leblanc flung himself backwards, and the weapon crashed down, clanging off the floor.

And then he jackknifed away as it arced toward him again.

He had moments to try and save his own life. This time, moving his hand in a blur, he tried to grab it as it landed on the steel, inches away from his belly.

He felt the shock, the surge of power that came from the man's energy, but he held on. Blocking the next blow, he pushed the man back, using his weight to keep him off balance.

And then, with a clang of metal, Katie rushed down the stairs.

"Drop that!" she yelled, aiming her gun at the man.

There was a sudden, shocked silence in the metal cave. All Leblanc could hear was their harsh breathing. With a jolt of fear, he wondered if the man would try to attack them both. If so, Katie's shot had better be accurate, because a ricochet down here would be lethal.

But then, their attacker lowered the axe and stood still. He seemed confused, though still aggressive. His face twisted with rage as he looked at the gun Katie was aiming at him, her hand steady.

"You shouldn't be in here," the man grunted, sounding furious.

Leblanc leaned over and grasped his gun, feeling a deep relief as the grip settled into his palm. He trained it on the man.

"Drop your weapon," Katie insisted sternly.

The axe clattered to the floor.

Katie took her flashlight out. It danced over the room, illuminating the serrated blades of a set of sharp looking knives on the wall. It illuminated the stain of blood on Leblanc's calf. His leg was throbbing in pain and he wasn't sure if he could walk.

It flashed over the man's angry face, and it highlighted the rusty, reddish stains that were dotted and splashed over his hands and forearms.

Blood, Katie thought, with a clench of her stomach.

"Are you Virgil Harvey? You're under arrest for multiple charges. Put your hands in front of you," she said, drawing the handcuffs off her belt.

Now, Virgil looked panicked.

"What are you doing? I thought you were robbers, man. I didn't know you were law enforcement," he gabbled. "I'm an innocent man. Just going about my business. You're the invaders here," he cried, his eyes wide and crazed.

"I identified myself clearly," Leblanc snapped at him. He couldn't believe the violence that had played out in this metal cave with its chemical smell and that sputtering lamp. Virgil Harvey was most definitely not entirely sane. Undoubtedly, he had no inhibition to try and kill.

He stood up, gasping in pain. His leg was in agony. Lurching forward, he grabbed Virgil's wrists while Katie cuffed him.

"You're under arrest, Virgil Harvey," Katie said calmly.

Leblanc bent down to clutch his bleeding, aching leg. But despite the pain, he was feeling a sense of triumph. They'd got their man at last. Now, they could question him.

CHAPTER TWENTY EIGHT

There was something seriously wrong with Virgil Harvey, Katie saw, as she watched him writhe and struggle against the cuffs that held him in his chair in the police interview room.

His wrists were so thick and broad that the handcuffs seemed flimsy in comparison. His fingernails were broken and dirty. And the man himself was off-the-scale weird in his behavior.

She'd had a hell of a time getting him along the corridor to this interview room after the team had removed him from the police van that had picked him up. It had taken three of them to wrestle him in here. And that was after getting the stinking, heavy coat and hat off him. Concealed in the clothing, they had found two different, jagged knives.

Now, she and Leblanc were in the interview room, but Katie feared that even with both of them there, questioning Virgil might not be possible.

He was shouting out in rage. Spittle flew from his mouth as he ranted.

"What you doing to me? What you doing to me? You got to let me go, and if you don't I'm going to hurt you, bad."

He was incoherent. Aggressive. He gave off a weird, evil energy, Katie thought. Although that wasn't only due to his agitation.

As soon as they had gone further into the container, they had discovered the underground site was home to a full-scale meth den. The doomstay prepper front had clearly concealed his real business.

Scott had helicoptered in detectives Clark and Anderson from the task force, to conduct a full search of the premises. They were going through the underground cabin, combing it for any trace evidence linked to the murders.

Johnson, the police psychologist who was part of the task force, had also arrived on site, and was watching from the observation room.

It was very clear that Virgil was high as a kite on his own stash and this would make the questioning a huge challenge. Katie had no doubt that was also the reason for the violent attack he'd launched on them.

Leblanc shifted into his seat with difficulty. He looked to be in intense pain and Katie was seriously worried about him. He needed hospital, X-rays and stitches. But he'd made do with disinfectant and a bandage from the first aid kit in the police department.

"Where were you earlier today?" she asked Virgil, trying to keep her voice calm.

"I was out hunting, man," he growled. "You don't understand. It's dangerous out there. I'm not the one. I'm not the one!"

"Where were you yesterday?" Leblanc asked. But Harvey didn't answer. Instead, he started struggling again, trying to break free from the cuffs, letting out roars of rage.

"I'm protecting my territory! People mustn't interfere with me. They must just leave me alone.

They thought they could stop me! No one can stop me! I will destroy them all!"

"Why did you attack me?" Leblanc asked loudly.

But he just went on raving. His skin was twitching as if things were crawling under it.

"You'll have to ask the man in the mask. He's the one who sent you, isn't he? He's the one. I saw him at the store."

"What store is this?" Leblanc asked, sounding at the end of his patience.

"The general store, man. You know, the place where I buy supplies," he screamed, his voice shrill with rage.

Leblanc shrugged.

"If you say so. But now, tell me, what's that on your arms?" he pressured. "I see stains there. They look like blood. They must be recent. What are they from?"

"Nothing, man. You got me twisted."

Katie leaned forward. "Tell us the truth," she insisted.

Something about this interview was feeling off-kilter. Weirdly, despite all the evidence, she was starting to doubt her own certainty that he was the killer. He was just too off-beat. Too far removed from reality.

"It's nothing. It's paint. I'm telling you, I'm not the one! People just mustn't come close to me. They must stay out of my territory. Stay away!"

Katie glanced at Leblanc. They were getting no sense from this man, but in his ranting it was clear that he was violent, dangerous and territorial. They'd have to send a pathologist in to take a swab from his arm. That evidence could be important.

But for the moment, their questions weren't getting answered. Katie stood up and so did Leblanc. Virgil let out a roar of laughter as he saw how lame and incapacitated her partner was as he limped to the door.

Outside, they met Johnson, who had rushed out of the observation room where he'd been watching with two of the local detectives.

"He's not making sense," Johnson admitted. "But that's due to the drugs. He's clearly got no inhibition to kill, and is fiercely protective about his territory."

Katie nodded. The territory was slap-bang in the middle of where the affected ranches were located.

"It's highly likely he could have perceived those tourists as somehow being a threat to him," Johnson added. "He mentioned hunting. That's what he could have been doing. In his own way."

"Can that blood on his arms be tested?" Katie asked.

"We're waiting for the pathologist to arrive and he'll take swabs," Johnson agreed. "But for now, I feel this is pretty much cut and dried. We have found our killer."

Katie took a deep breath.

"I disagree," she said. "I don't think we can say that without DNA proof. At first, I also thought he was. But now, I'm doubting myself and rethinking."

As she'd expected, the men swiveled around to stare at her as if she was mad. Leblanc was glowering.

"What? Why not?" Leblanc demanded.

"He's high on meth. He's out of control. He's not making any sense."

"Yes?" Leblanc looked at her challengingly, as if to say 'and your point is?'

"That's not this killer's mindset. He planned this. He waited and observed patiently for hours to get the targets he needed, and he chose them carefully. This suspect can't sit still for five seconds and he's not thinking logically."

"The fact he's high is a vital piece of the puzzle," Leblanc insisted.

"But it doesn't fit. It doesn't feel right," Katie said.

Leblanc gave her a hard stare.

"There is literally nobody else who is so well located, who has shown eagerness to kill, and who has a strong motive for protecting his territory."

"It's not him. I wish it was, but I feel it's not," Katie insisted. "If the DNA evidence on his arms links up with one of the victims, I'll change my mind, but not until then."

"He's high at this time. It's impossible to say what he'd be like in a normal state," Johnson argued.

Katie shook her head. " He's clearly a habitual user and this means the behavior we see now, is what he is. Irrational. Impulsive. Aggressive, sure, but he's not going to be able to plan."

"So, where does that leave us?" Leblanc asked, frustrated.

"We've still got to keep looking," Katie insisted.

"All of this evidence is against him," Johnson argued. "Evidence is what will lead the jury. This is a slam dunk case."

Katie felt frustration boil inside her, the more so because she could see their argument. He did seem to be the likely killer. Circumstantially, there was no doubt that he could have done it.

Even the psychologist on the team was convinced.

Katie was alone in her opinion that a serial killer needed to be more organized, more cold minded and thoughtful, more of a planner, to do what this murderer had done.

Perhaps she was wrong, she thought suddenly. What if she was clinging to a preconception that wasn't true in this case? Killers were diverse in their warped mentality. She didn't want to compromise the investigation if every other person thought differently.

But she found herself shaking her head stubbornly. Her experience and intuition would not allow her to back down.

"I'm sorry," she said. "Arrest him for meth possession and dealing. Arrest him for attacking an officer of the law. But I just can't see him as a serial murderer. I think you're going to test that blood and find it belongs to an animal, something he hunted."

Leblanc sighed.

Yet again they were in conflict.

"We will have to start from scratch to find a new suspect. We are all out of leads and all out of time," he said, sounding exasperated. "You know what pressure we're under from the authorities. Scott has already organized a media conference to take place later this evening."

The others were looking at her.

"The knife didn't look familiar, either," Katie said, remembering the original glimpse she'd had as her attacker had brandished it.

"Are you sure about that?" Johnson pressured her. "You only saw that blade for a moment, on a dark night, when he attacked you. You might have misremembered what you saw, or else he could have hidden the murder weapon somewhere else."

"He's right," Leblanc said.

Before Katie could retaliate, her phone started ringing.

It was Scott on the line, she saw. Now she felt even more conflicted. He must be calling to congratulate her and the team. And here she was, arguing that the suspect they'd arrested was not the man they were looking for.

With a sigh, Katie picked up the call.

"Afternoon, Scott," she said, switching the phone to speaker so the others could hear.

His voice thrummed with tension.

"Katie. I don't know what's going on here. I thought you had a suspect in custody?"

"We do," she said, feeling a thrill of dread in the pit of her stomach. She saw the faces of the others change, looking guarded and apprehensive at his tone

"I've just had another murder called in. From Pine Ridge, which is a ranch in northern Montana, on the border with Canada. Exactly the same M.O. Police have just arrived on the scene."

Now, they all exchanged shocked glances.

"Could it be an older body, recently discovered?" Leblanc asked.

"It's a new kill. That's the first thing I asked. It's not more than a couple of hours old. I need you to get there, now. I thought this case was over, finished, closed. But he's still out there and this is now a disaster."

CHAPTER TWENTY NINE

Pine Ridge Ranch was a half-hour drive from the small police precinct where they'd been interviewing Virgil. Katie flattened her foot as the SUV sped through the snowy landscape, eating up the miles.

"You were right," Leblanc said flatly from the passenger seat.

"I wish I wasn't," Katie replied.

Leblanc was silent for a while. Then he took a deep breath.

"Sorry I doubted you," he said.

Katie gave a tiny shrug. Leblanc's apology offered a shred of comfort and confidence in this tense situation.

If only they had kept on looking, and not spent so much time and resources in questioning Virgil Harvey. They'd thought they had the correct suspect, but if she'd had her doubts earlier, then potentially, a life could have been saved, Katie thought, feeling bitter remorse.

Ahead, she saw the tall wooden gateposts of Pine Ridge appear before them. A police car was stopped outside the gateway, its lights flashing. Beyond, Katie saw a series of luxurious-looking log cabins strung out across a valley.

She leaned out the driver's door and called to the police officer.

"Winter and Leblanc from the special task force."

He nodded grimly. "Follow me."

The police SUV headed into the ranch, veering from the paved path to bump along a snowy trail. The track wound through scattered pine forest before Katie saw the lights of another car ahead, and a small knot of people at the crime scene.

Feeling dread chill her stomach, she climbed out.

The police officer jumped out of his car, briefing her and Leblanc in a low voice as they trudged over the packed snow to the scene.

"It's exactly the same M.O. as the others," he said heavily. "Victim was found with a slashed throat, and marks to the face that are similar to a mauling. The body was dragged off the track a couple of yards and roughly covered in branches and snow. The crime is very recent. It probably occurred just over an hour ago."

"Who is the victim?" Katie asked.

"He's a sixty-five-year old man, Evan Parr."

“What happened?” Leblanc asked. “How was he found?”

“He was cross-country skiing with his wife when he injured his knee and was unable to walk. She went back for help. On the way, a neighbor, hunting in the woods, noticed her alone and escorted her back to the ranch. He’d heard about the killings and was concerned to see her alone. If he hadn’t gone to help her, who knows? We could be dealing with two victims," he said. "She told us she had a feeling she was being followed. By the time she got back to the scene an hour later, with a ranch hand and a medic, as well as the neighbor, her husband had been killed, and his body moved a few yards off the track."

Chills rushed down Katie's spine. The killer had been alert, watching. Ready to pounce on someone he knew for sure couldn’t fight back.

The timeframe proved that Virgil Harvey could not possible be the killer. He was already in police custody when this victim had been murdered.

Taking a deep breath, she stepped forward.

A yard away, covered in snow, was the body, hands and face mauled, slashed throat gaping. His sightless eyes were wide. The snow around him was stained red.

"Weren't these people warned?" Katie asked softly. "Didn't the ranch warn them?"

The officer nodded. "They were 'advised' to go out in a group but this ranch didn't want to panic guests by enforcing the policy. The owner said he thought it would never happen here, that the chances were far too small. And they did head out as a pair. I guess they never thought one of them would be injured.”

Undoubtedly this was the same killer, Katie saw. Even the terrain was as she'd expected to see, with tracts of forest close by and the trail winding between the trees. This was the killing ground that he seemed to seek out.

Again, she thought to herself how familiar he seemed to be with the area, and with the way the ranches were set up.

"No sign of a struggle," the police officer explained.

It had been quick and brutal. Like the others had been. The way he would have killed Katie, too, if she hadn't fought back.

"Any indication of which way he fled?" she asked.

Apart from the body, the only other evidence visible nearby was the scattered pine needles and branches.

"There are rough tracks nearby but they lead into the woods and we lost the trail there," the police officer said. "We think he had a snowmobile or a car parked at an access point near the road, but there are numerous access points along this road. We're searching, though. Going through all of them."

She knew that investigators would be sweeping the entire area, and that they would follow up on any footprints. But so far that line of investigation had not produced results.

She turned to Leblanc.

"I feel we're missing something," she said.

"What would that be?" he asked.

"I'm not sure. But I feel we need to go back to our original thinking, and approach this logically. I think we're overlooking an important fact."

"What's that?"

Katie paced away from the scene, back down the trail, as she thought out loud.

"This killer is close to these businesses. Close to this area. But he's not targeting the businesses themselves."

"Yes, he is," Leblanc protested, sounding surprised. "That's exactly what he's targeting. That's why the ranches are all suffering now, and we're under so much pressure."

"Yes, but he is specifically targeting the people. The guests. His kills are up close and personal. I think that's where his hatred lies. And that means he must have been close to one of those businesses in the past. In fact, I have a strong feeling he was close to all of them. He must have a reason to hold a grudge against the clientele. Which means he was an employee there, correct?"

"That's a jump. We've already eliminated that theory earlier," Leblanc argued.

"No. I disagree. We didn't explore it deeply enough," Katie retorted.

"What do you think we missed?"

“We didn’t go back far enough. We couldn’t have done that at the time based on the fact only two ranches were hit when we looked at the employee records. Going back more than a few months seemed like a waste of time. But now it’s clear to me that this killer must have a deep history with the area. A longer history than we assumed.”

"So where are you at with this?" Leblanc asked.

"We have a lot more information now. We know this killer is from this area. He has to be. He lives locally. He is extremely familiar with all the shortcuts and getaway points. And he must have worked on the ranches. Maybe he's a kitchen hand, an assistant, a cleaner. A person with access to everything, and someone who knows the ins and outs of each business. But whoever he is, in his mind, he has a reason to hate the people who come here. And that tells us something!"

Leblanc frowned. "I see your logic. I understand that line of thought. But I'm worried, Katie, because the evidence might also play a role here. This trail is as fresh as it will ever be. We should be driving around and hunting through all the access points, to track down his vehicle, where he parked, and where he went."

Katie shrugged.

"Okay. You do that. I'm going to hunt down his history in the area, go back further, work more thoroughly. Look for someone who was close to every affected ranch."

"That makes sense. We're covering both bases," Leblanc agreed.

"You join the search, and I'll take the car. I'll base myself at the police department, call around to the other ranches to get a full history, and then head out immediately if I find anything solid."

She hoped that her theory would pan out, because Katie knew that neither of them could afford for the killer to escape again.

That colossal failure would jeopardize the future of the entire task team at the worst possible time, with the media conference already set up and taking place this evening. She had to have faith in her logic, and hope that she could uncover the trail that would lead her to the killer this time.

CHAPTER THIRTY

"A disgruntled employee," Katie said to herself, feeling determination rise inside her again as the first of the records she'd asked for came through. "But not a recent one. Someone who's been involved with the area for years. Who's hopped from job to job, maybe with breaks in between. But who shows a pattern of unwanted behavior that gets him fired every time."

Her profiler's instincts told her she was on the right track with this.

She was working from the local police department's back office. It was crowded with paper, but a small desk had been cleared for them. In the corner, a heater rattled. The walls were papered with yellowing notifications, and newer laminated posters.

She was the only person in the back office, because all the others were out on the hunt.

Katie barely noticed her surroundings. All her focus was on who the killer could be. Opening her laptop, she scrolled through all the evidence she had collected so far.

She knew she was tired. It was late in the afternoon and getting dark, and she had been working all day on a hard and dangerous case. But she couldn't afford to be tired now. She had to keep her mind sharp or an important detail might be overlooked.

"He's patient. He watches," she told herself. "He knows the layout of ranches and how they work. He knows where the tracks are, and how to hide in the woods."

What did that mean? Murmuring as she worked, she took her logic a step further.

"He seems obsessed with taking a grudge out on the wealthy clientele. That means he must have a reason to resent them, in his mind at least. So, what if he was fired for that? For peeking at guests? That would be a real problem in this caliber of business, catering for top-end visitors. And it would show who he was. Antisocial. Obsessed with them in an unhealthy way."

Excitement surged in Katie as she thought about that possibility.

She was going to go back further this time. Two years should do it. That would show her the bigger picture of how this killer had been intertwined with the ranches and guests he targeted.

Why would he have waited before starting to kill?

There could be many reasons, Katie surmised.

He could have gone to jail for a while, imprisoned for a few months for petty crime. He could have been injured and had to wait until his injury healed. Perhaps he moved away from the area and came back home when he was fired yet again. Or perhaps he was simply waiting for the depths of winter, when the snow would be thickest and there would be the best chance of covering his tracks.

Or else, something totally different might have triggered his killing instinct, because that was sometimes how it worked.

Of course, all of this meant nothing if she couldn't find who he was.

Anxiously, she scanned the records from Diamond Ice Ranch, which had been the first to arrive. She saw Maple Ranch was also in her inbox.

She started to work her way through the records, reading the names of the people who had been fired or who had left or moved on.

Katie felt certain now that they had given up on this theory too early. With only two affected ranches the first time they had rightly believed that the issues triggering the killer would have had to be recent. But now, as the bigger picture unfolded and more ranches were affected, she knew there was a longer and more complex history to be discovered.

However, there didn't seem to be anything in common between these first two places, and Katie felt anxiety twist inside her at the thought her theory was wrong. She was looking for something specific, and she just wasn't seeing it.

Katie sighed in defeat after rereading the list again. Comparing the two ranches, her theory had already been disproved. She simply couldn't believe it.

There were no employees in common, going back two years, that had been fired. She didn't see a single name appear on both the lists.

At that moment, her phone rang. It was the manager of Diamond Ice.

"Agent Katie Winter?" he asked.

"Speaking. I received the information," she said, feeling stressed that it hadn't been useful.

But then he spoke again.

"I realized just after I sent it, that it wasn't complete. We took over some staff from a ranch that closed. One of them was a problem almost immediately and we let him go while still in the trial period and before he was on our system. That was about two years ago. I'm not sure if that's going too far back?"

"What were the circumstances?" Katie asked. "And his name?"

"He was a handyman and maintenance person but he didn't respect guest privacy. He would wander around the ranch, peeking in windows at the guests. It was like he was obsessed with them. he was fired after a family complained about him. When we confronted him, he lost his temper. I guess he just took it badly. He started yelling, and caused such a commotion we had to call security to remove him. His name is Barton Caulfield," the manager said.

Katie thought that this little room suddenly seemed a whole lot brighter.

What did he look like? Do you recall?" she asked.

"He was average height, maybe five-nine, five-ten. Well built, a strong guy. I remember thinking when we had the complaint, that it was strange because he seemed ordinary and harmless. He was very good with his hands. An excellent handyman. Clever. But the problem was significant so we had to let him go."

"Thank you so much for telling me this. It could be very important. Do you know where he lives?"

The manager paused. "I know he lived very close by. I can try and look up his address details."

"I'd appreciate that. What you've given me has been such a help," Katie said. At least his place of residence was now narrowed down.

Now that she had this information, as well as three more sets of records from other ranches, Katie felt she was getting somewhere.

She found Barton Caulfield's name linked to Maple Ranch and Pine Ridge Ranch as well as Caribou Wilderness Resort. He'd been fired from Maple Ranch eight months ago after being rude to a guest. Katie wondered if the rudeness had included peering through windows. And he'd been fired from Caribou three months ago. He'd gotten into a fight with another employee. He'd injured the other employee with a knife. In the struggle, he'd had his arm broken badly.

There was the reason for the delayed revenge, Katie decided.

Whatever the case, she was learning more about him all the time. And now she had enough evidence to be certain that this was the killer.

He was the only person she'd found who had been fired from all of them. And he was living some distance from the ranches. He might not have had to travel far to get to each location. He was the right age. He was the right build. He was working his way through his list of targets.

How could she pinpoint where he stayed?

One of the ranches must know. They would have noted it down in their employee records. Perhaps not Diamond Ice, as he was never on their system, but the others would for sure.

Katie sent an email back to all of them, marked Urgent.

"Do you have an address for ex-employee Barton Caulfield? Please send it asap."

She waited, watching the screen, deciding she would give it five minutes before picking up the phone and seeing if that went faster.

But almost immediately, her inbox pinged.

There were two incoming mails, from Caribou Wilderness Resort and Maple Ranch.

Both said the same thing:

"Barton Caulfield's last known address is 35 Outpost Road."

She looked again at the map, and saw that this address was in the local area. It was very close to the Canadian border, although further west than they had imagined. He must have started out applying to the closest ranch, and then made his way gradually further and further east, she decided.

There was no guarantee he would still be there, but Katie suspected that based on his mindset and habits, he would have stayed where he was, to ensure familiarity with his hunting ground.

Quickly, she messaged Leblanc to tell him where she was headed.

Then she climbed in her car, hoping that this time, she would end up on the killer's doorstep.

CHAPTER THIRTY ONE

The drive took longer than Katie had expected. The area she was heading into was rough and mountainous, and a fallen tree blocked one of the roads, forcing her to backtrack and reroute.

Here it was. Her headlights cut the dark, with bright snowflakes fluttering down from an overhanging branch as she turned.

She felt tense and expectant as she saw the small wooden cabin at the end of the rutted, snowy drive.

Katie parked her car and got out, her breath pluming out in front of her as she stood, staring towards the cabin. There was no sign of movement there, and she saw no lights. The place looked deserted. But there was a lean-to behind the cabin and she saw the shape of a vehicle parked under it.

She held her gun in her hand as she paced toward the building, moving slowly, listening hard.

Finally, she was standing outside the wooden door.

She knocked loudly.

“Police! Open up!” she yelled, and listened, heart pounding, to the resounding silence that followed.

Then, something caught her eye. A rusty red smudge on the wood, near the handle. Adrenaline surged as she picked it up.

This was no time for hesitation. Not when they had a killer to catch.

With her left hand, Katie wrenched the door handle and shoved it hard.

It flew open, and she burst inside.

"Police!" she shouted again, but was met with silence. She saw a small room, with a table and two chairs, a fireplace, an ancient kettle on the counter, and another door beyond that must lead to the bedroom.

There was a faint smell of smoke.

"Barton Caulfield?" she called out again, and again, there was silence.

And then, she saw it. Lying on the workbench on the side of the room.

It was a strange, clumsy looking knife, with a frayed leather handle and a twisted, serrated blade still dark with blood. Katie felt her mouth go dry as she stared at what was undoubtedly the murder weapon. It had to be.

She stepped toward it, and then from behind her, she heard the tiniest hint of movement.

Katie whirled around. In a moment, she saw she was confronting her attacker for the second time.

She caught a horrifying glimpse of the now-familiar sight of that knife's twisted blade as he slashed at her. Gasping in a breath, she managed to jerk out of the way, raising her gun. But in the small, gloomy space, as she steadied herself to take the shot, she stumbled back over one of the chairs. Her gun muzzle jerked wide, and then there was no time. Desperately, she hit the ground as the knife flashed toward her again.

His harsh breathing resounded in the small room as he leaped forward again. His eyes were strangely piercing and intense in the dim light. Katie rolled to the side, this time, feeling the blade tear through her jacket. This man was so quick. He used the weapon as if it was a part of him. At close quarters, a knife could be just as deadly as a gun, and she hadn't had the chance to get a clear shot at him.

She writhed back, under the table, knowing she had to try because each attack represented a deadly risk. But in the close quarters of the cabin she couldn't risk a ricochet.

The knife flashed again and she ducked out of the way, hearing it crack down against the table. Katie glanced around, looking for something she could use to fend off his attack. At least, for as long as it took to get a clear shot. One of the chairs would work. She grabbed the flimsy chair and flung it at him.

It clattered onto his shoulder and he shoved it aside. But that had given her some distance between them and it had slowed down his attack.

Finally, she had the space and time to plan a clear shot at him. She brought her gun around as quick as she could and pulled the trigger. The sound was shockingly loud in the small room.

He reacted instantly he saw the gun, leaping to the right as she fired. She missed, and the bullet went wide.

But it was clear that Barton was not up for the fight. In fact, Katie now saw recognition in his eyes as he gazed at her. He'd realized who she was. Even as she aimed again, he retreated. He turned, ducked, and fled out of the door.

Scrambling to her feet, Katie rushed to the doorway. She paused, listening, not wanting to race straight in an ambush if he was lurking there and hoping to disarm her.

She leaped out, spinning around to cover all angles, aware that at close quarters, a knife could be almost as lethal as a gun.

But there was no sign of Barton.

He was gone. Cursing, Katie ran into the snow, with the wind whipping at her face. Where were his tracks?

There they were, deep in the snow, heading toward the tree line.

She plunged after him, adrenaline surging as she headed into the darkness. Her ears were straining to pick up the slightest sound of his running footsteps.

The trail was clear until she reached the forest. But inside, to her bitter disappointment, she lost him.

The trees were thick and dark around her, and the snow was uneven and distressed on the ground. She had no doubt that he knew the best way through these trees, and had been able to cover his tracks once he was inside their shelter.

Disgusted with herself, she cast around, breathing hard. This had been an abject failure.

She'd had the killer cornered, she'd had him in her sights, and she'd failed to catch him.

For the second time, they had physically fought and he'd gotten away.

Unwilling to give up, she doggedly battled on. Scrambling over branches and pushing through leaves, she hoped that she could pick up the trail again as she tried to predict which direction he would have fled.

Katie moved deeper into the forest. There was no way he could have fled far. She kept listening out for any trace of him, but the wind was not her friend, whistling noisily through the leaves and rattling the branches.

At that moment, her phone rang.

It was Leblanc.

"Katie. What's happening?" he said urgently. "I've just arrived here."

"I got him," she said breathlessly. "But he got away. That was his cabin, but I was too slow. I've lost his tracks in the woods. We need to set up a search."

"I'll call for backup," Leblanc said. "And I'll start searching from this side, in case he doubles back."

"But you're injured," Katie protested. "You should stay in the car. You won't be able to chase him, and you'll risk permanently damaging your leg." She felt worried at the thought of her partner doing himself serious harm.

"I'm fine," Leblanc said. "I'm not an invalid. I can manage. In any case, I'm calling for backup now."

She could hear the trademark stubbornness in his voice before he disconnected, and she returned her focus to thinking where Barton might have gone.

She couldn't just cast around, hoping to pick up his tracks. The terrain was too complicated and he would have found a way to confuse her.

If she were him, where would she go?

Would he make a straight line for the next road, or would he try to circle back? Breathing deeply, she tried to think like him. What would he do to throw her off course?

And then, to her horror, she realized what he would do.

He would double back. He would not run blindly. Not when he had a car to use. He'd want to get away, as fast and far as he could, using his wheels.

So he would return to the cabin. That was what he'd planned.

The problem was that he would find Leblanc there.

An injured man, with a seriously compromised leg. Just like the last victim he'd killed. A man who was driving a car belonging to one of the local ranches, that would not attract any suspicion if Barton took it and drove it away.

Horror filling her, Katie could imagine the scenario playing out as Barton took action. He would not hesitate because he would perceive Leblanc to be weak and incapacitated. That was what he was looking for now. Targets he perceived as easy.

Leblanc was in serious danger, and she needed to get back through the woods as fast as she could, to prevent what she feared would happen.

CHAPTER THIRTY TWO

Leblanc stopped the car and stared at the small cabin ahead. This was the killer's lair. At last they'd tracked him to his home, but the biggest challenge and danger still lay ahead. Barton Caulfield was a cunning, dangerous adversary.

Now that he was here, Leblanc decided to hole up out of sight, so that if Barton returned, he would walk straight into an ambush.

The guy had fled on foot, so he would surely need to come back to collect money, possessions, or even transport - he saw a lean-to behind the cabin where he guessed a vehicle was housed.

He'd be back fast, Leblanc decided. He'd know that the police were closing in, and that he had to act immediately to save himself.

He climbed out of the car and almost fell on his face in the snow. Pain lanced up his leg. He'd downplayed the injury, needing to help Katie at this critical time, but damn, it hurt so much he could barely put weight on it.

Reaching back into the car, he grasped the walking stick that the ranch manager had thoughtfully given him as a temporary measure when he'd seen how hurt he was.

Leaning on the stick, he gritted his teeth and hobbled toward the cabin door. The lean-to itself would be the best place to hide. Then he could stay out of sight and would have the element of total surprise.

He gritted his teeth, concentrating on his breathing, trying to ignore his weak leg as he pushed onward.

The snow was treacherous, and he didn't want to fall and injure himself further. Truthfully, he was in no fit state to be chasing anyone. But he had to do this. He just had to.

It was only a few yards, but each step was agony. His leg protested with every stride.

And then, as he passed the cabin door, to his shock, it burst open.

Leblanc turned, adrenaline surging inside him as a man in a dark parka burst out of the small cabin.

In a flash, Leblanc realized he was two steps behind. The killer had already circled back and had been waiting. And Leblanc hadn't yet drawn his gun.

Before he could do so much as grab it, the man was on him, the sharp, twisted blade of his knife gleaming dully in the faint light. He could see his pale fingers, tightly gripping the leather-wrapped handle.

Leblanc raised his good hand to defend himself, knowing that he had only a split second to fight back. He caught the arm and twisted it, using all of his strength to knock the blade away. His opponent was strong, though, and his arm was solid muscle. Leblanc dodged sideways, desperately trying to avoid the slashing blade as it struck again.

With a surge of panic, he acknowledged that he was the weaker, the slower one, and this man was the hunter.

Desperately, Leblanc jabbed the walking cane at the man, trying to disarm him. But the man dodged, kicking Leblanc hard in his bad leg, causing him to fall backwards with a yell of pain.

The killer tackled him, and Leblanc caught sight of his face, twisted and distorted into a mask of anger and hatred as he thrust the knife down, aiming to sink it into Leblanc's chest.

He grabbed the attacker's arm, trying to hold off the blade, but the man was too strong.

The knife caught his shoulder, tearing through his coat and shirt, narrowly missing skewering him as he jackknifed his body away.

He needed to get to his gun, but he couldn't, because he was now pinned on his side in the snow, and it was taking both hands and all his strength to keep this attacker from murdering him. The man was frighteningly strong and fast.

Frantic, Leblanc rolled away, trying to buy himself some time, but cat-quick, the man followed. The blade raised high, ready to strike.

If he didn't do something soon he was going to die, here, in the frozen wilderness, just like the poor woman, who had suffered and died alone, butchered by this psychotic bastard.

Desperate, Leblanc grabbed the man's wrist, trying to hold it back, away from him. He clawed at the weapon, trying to get the blade off him.

The man was panting, grunting with the effort, but he was using his weight and the strength of his body to crush Leblanc's hands, preventing him from getting a grip on him.

And then, with a growl of fury, the killer managed to put his foot into Leblanc's chest, thrusting him back, away from him.

Making a grab for his leg, Leblanc tried to shift his weight to roll them both, to knock the killer into the snow and disarm him.

He knew that if he didn't gain the upper hand, he was going to die.

The man followed his roll, and Leblanc tried to grasp the man's wrist, but he was flung off balance, falling into the snow, pain shooting through his damaged leg. He was so close to getting to his gun. All he needed was one moment, one lucky break, and he'd have it.

But the killer was too fast, too strong. This time, Leblanc realized that he was well and truly in trouble.

No way could he fight off this attacker. He had to move his damaged leg to reach his gun, and he couldn't do it from this position, in this deep snow.

He saw in the man's eyes, the same feral look he'd seen on the faces of killers before. There was no remorse. No thought of the consequences. Only a focused, lethal desire to kill.

He heard the man whisper, "I'm going to kill you.

The words were almost a growl, and the man's breath was hot on his face.

He looked ready to strike. By the look of his eyes, he was going to relish the moment. The knife was coming for his neck, and the angle was all wrong for him to try and fight it.

And then, from behind him, he heard the explosion of a gun.

The man staggered back, a look of surprise on his face as the blade dropped from his hand.

Blood seeped through the man's shirt sleeve, and he stared down at it in horror.

Leblanc had only time to think what a brilliant shot that was, a direct hit exactly where it needed to be in order to disable his attacker the fastest.

And then he lunged forward, grabbing the man's legs and yanking him off balance so that he stumbled and fell hard in the slippery snow.

Katie rushed up, gun in hand, aiming it at Barton's head.

"Don't get up! Hands in the air!" she ordered.

Barton's face twisted with hatred, his eyes glittering with rage. But he had no choice. Reluctantly, he raised his hands. Blood seeped from his right sleeve. The bullet had pierced him just below the elbow.

"You're under arrest," Katie informed him breathlessly. "Barton Caulfield, we're arresting you on suspicion of multiple counts of murder and other charges.

Struggling to his feet, gasping and leaning on the walking stick, Leblanc got on his phone and called for medical backup. The suspect was injured, and would need to go straight to the hospital under police guard.

Leblanc resolved he was going to make personally sure that the security surrounding the killer was as tight as it could be, so that he had no chance of escape until he was safely locked in a maximum security cell.

He felt deeply relieved and saw that Katie shared his emotions.

As he looked into her eyes, it caught him, low down in his belly, making him feel almost breathless as he realized during this case, each of them had saved the other's life.

They'd caught the man who had ravaged the area, causing fear and loss.

Finally, this case was solved.

CHAPTER THIRTY THREE

Katie watched anxiously as Leblanc limped out of the hospital at Sault Ste Marie, leaning on a crutch. But he was smiling.

"X-rays are done. No bones broken," he said. "Just a badly strained muscle that's all wrapped up, and a deep but clean wound needing eight stitches. And lots of painkillers."

"You're as tough as nails," she said, pleased that her partner had escaped serious injury.

"Tough? I'm a real softie. Like a marshmallow." He grinned at her, and she knew he was teasing her.

"It could have been a lot worse. The entire outcome could have," she said, more seriously.

"At least Barton Caulfield is in prison now," he said, checking the message that Scott had just sent before going into the press conference.

"Yes. That's a relief. Suspects in hospital always worry me," Katie said as they got into the car. "It's too easy to escape from a hospital, even under police guard. But now that he's been transferred to maximum-security, he'll be going nowhere except the courtroom. Multiple life sentences, for sure, for what he's done."

"Glad to hear it."

With minor difficulty, Leblanc lifted his leg inside and closed the door.

"It's very late, but there are still a couple of places open. Want to grab a drink? And a bite to eat?" he asked.

"Sure," Katie said. "Let's go."

Strangely, she felt there was still a slight tension between them as she started up the car.

Confirming her suspicions, Leblanc cleared his throat.

"I want to apologize," he said, sounding surprisingly meek.

"You do?" she asked, surprised.

"I – I shouldn't have laid into you the way I did, after you went out on your own and he nearly killed you. I overreacted. It was wrong of me."

"No, no. You reminded me of very important priorities," Katie protested, but Leblanc wasn't done yet.

“I didn’t want anything to happen to you. I feel that after my last case partner, I – I’d never be able to get close to an investigation partner again. But I feel we’re close. We work damned well together. And it would be terrible to lose you,” he concluded, with an expressive shrug.

Katie felt her face start getting warm. What Leblanc had said meant a lot. She realized that for years, she hadn’t let herself get close to anyone, either. And she was getting close to him. That was why his anger had hurt so badly.

“I appreciate what you said. I feel the same,” she admitted.

But before they pulled off, he surprised her again.

"You know, a while ago, you mentioned that you wanted me to help me with your sister's case?"

"Yes. I did." She waited, feeling nervous and expectant.

“Do you want to reopen it? If so, we should do that now.”

Katie took a deep breath, gripping the wheel, because this was a potentially life changing decision. "Leblanc, I do. I want to relook at it. I want to understand what happened and read through the entire file. I was just a kid when it happened. I was an innocent, small-town sixteen-year-old who was totally traumatized by it all. I have no idea if all the correct processes were followed, or if there was other evidence I didn't know about."

He nodded. "Are you sure you're ready for it?"

It was a sensible question.

"I'm sure that I need to know the exact details of what happened, if I'm ever going to move on and forget about it, and try to live my life. And if there are any omissions or irregularities, I want to explore them."

"It’s probably not going to be easy. You might learn things you never knew or suspected before."

"I understand that. But I still want to know. I need to know," Katie said.

"Okay then. Let's request that it gets reopened, and see what we can come up with," Leblanc said.

She felt a sense of excitement about what lay ahead. She was ready to take her life back, and put the past behind her, and she had Leblanc, the partner she trusted with her life, in her corner to do it with her.

But before she could do that, there was one crucial issue that she needed to confront.

*

The next morning, Katie stood again outside the front door of her childhood home. It was a freezing morning and the wind whipped her hair under the woolen hat.

She felt as if she'd come full circle. Here she was again. But this time, knowing she had Leblanc's support, she was able to push past the pain.

She knocked firmly on the door, knowing that at least one of her parents must be home, because the small pickup was parked in the garage. Once again, she felt the familiar emotions start to crush her.

Anger.

Betrayal.

Confusion.

And she knew that if she didn't resolve the situation, it would slowly eat away at her.

She'd doubted herself, and her ability to deal with this. But she'd made the decision to come here, and now she'd have to see it through, no matter what happened next.

Nobody was answering the front door, and for a moment, she wanted to scream at her mother, her father, and the ghosts of her childhood.

Instead, she started walking around the side of the house, feeling the cold seeping into her bones.

She walked all the way around to the small, snow-covered backyard, with its straggling grass pushing through the snow, and neglected herb garden. The small shed where she and her sister had played was now locked up tight.

Katie found herself looking up at the upstairs window of her old room. That was where she and Josie had slept. Even up to the age of sixteen, they'd shared a room. They'd shared so much. But were there things she still didn't know?

She approached the side door, which led into the kitchen.

She tried the knob. Unlocked. As always.

She pushed, the door slightly ajar, the wood swollen with damp, and stuck.

If they wouldn't come out to her, then she would go to them. She felt ready.

This time, no matter what it took, she was going to break the silence.

Taking a deep breath, she walked inside the house.

NOW AVAILABLE!

BELIEVE ME
(A Katie Winter FBI Suspense Thriller—Book 4)

A dangerous killer makes his way north from Denver, heading for the upper reaches of Canada and leaving a trail of victims in his wake, all caught in his signature macabre traps. The FBI needs Special Agent Katie Winter to team up with her elite cross-border team to hunt him down—but in the remote northern regions of Canada, will this diabolical hunter lead her straight into a trap?

"Molly Black has written a taut thriller that will keep you on the edge of your seat... I absolutely loved this book and can't wait to read the next book in the series!"
—Reader review for Girl One: Murder

BELIEVE ME is book #4 in a new series by #1 bestselling mystery and suspense author Molly Black.

FBI Special Agent Katie Winter is no stranger to frigid winters, isolation, and dangerous cases. With her sterling record of hunting down serial killers, she is a fast-rising star in the BAU, and Katie is the natural choice to partner with Canadian law enforcement to track killers across brutal and unforgiving landscapes.

Yet this time, she may have just met her match.

A complex psychological crime thriller full of twists and turns and packed with heart-pounding suspense, the KATIE WINTER mystery series will make you fall in love with a brilliant new female protagonist and keep you turning pages late into the night.

Books #5 and #6 in the series—HELP ME and FORGET ME—are now also available.

"I binge read this book. It hooked me in and didn't stop till the last few pages… I look forward to reading more!"
—Reader review for Found You

"I loved this book! Fast-paced plot, great characters and interesting insights into investigating cold cases. I can't wait to read the next book!"
—Reader review for Girl One: Murder

"Very good book… You will feel like you are right there looking for the kidnapper! I know I will be reading more in this series!"
—Reader review for Girl One: Murder

"This is a very well written book and holds your interest from page 1… Definitely looking forward to reading the next one in the series, and hopefully others as well!"
—Reader review for Girl One: Murder

"Wow, I cannot wait for the next in this series. Starts with a bang and just keeps going."
—Reader review for Girl One: Murder

"Well written book with a great plot, one that will keep you up at night. A page turner!"
—Reader review for Girl One: Murder

"A great suspense that keeps you reading… can't wait for the next in this series!"
—Reader review for Found You

"Sooo soo good! There are a few unforeseen twists… I binge read this like I binge watch Netflix. It just sucks you in."
—Reader review for Found You

Molly Black

Bestselling author Molly Black is author of the MAYA GRAY FBI suspense thriller series, comprising nine books (and counting); the RYLIE WOLF FBI suspense thriller series, comprising six books (and counting); of the TAYLOR SAGE FBI suspense thriller series, comprising three books (and counting); and of the KATIE WINTER FBI suspense thriller series, comprising six books (and counting).

An avid reader and lifelong fan of the mystery and thriller genres, Molly loves to hear from you, so please feel free to visit www.mollyblackauthor.com to learn more and stay in touch.

BOOKS BY MOLLY BLACK

MAYA GRAY MYSTERY SERIES

GIRL ONE: MURDER (Book #1)
GIRL TWO: TAKEN (Book #2)
GIRL THREE: TRAPPED (Book #3)
GIRL FOUR: LURED (Book #4)
GIRL FIVE: BOUND (Book #5)
GIRL SIX: FORSAKEN (Book #6)
GIRL SEVEN: CRAVED (Book #7)
GIRL EIGHT: HUNTED (Book #8)
GIRL NINE: GONE (Book #9)

RYLIE WOLF FBI SUSPENSE THRILLER

FOUND YOU (Book #1)
CAUGHT YOU (Book #2)
SEE YOU (Book #3)
WANT YOU (Book #4)
TAKE YOU (Book #5)
DARE YOU (Book #6)

TAYLOR SAGE FBI SUSPENSE THRILLER

DON'T LOOK (Book #1)
DON'T BREATHE (Book #2)
DON'T RUN (Book #3)

KATIE WINTER FBI SUSPENSE THRILLER

SAVE ME (Book #1)
REACH ME (Book #2)
HIDE ME (Book #3)
BELIEVE ME (Book #4)
HELP ME (Book #5)
FORGET ME (Book #6)